Praise for the writing of Tere Michaels

Duty & Devotion

"It's sweet, it's endearing, it's well-developed, and the characters are awesomely human and real. Go read it. You'll be glad you did."

– *You Gotta Read Reviews*

"*Duty and Devotion* is a supremely satisfying conclusion to the story begun in *Love and Loyalty*."

– *Two Lips Reviews*

Love & Loyalty

"Highly recommended and definitely a keeper."

– *Reviews by Jessewave*

This is a fantastic story…"

– *Literary Nymphs*

Faith & Fidelity

"*Faith and Fidelity* is truly a moving masterpiece by a gifted author."

-- Kimberly Spinney, *Ecataromance*

"…*Faith & Fidelity* deserves a Gold Star Award."

-- Marcy Arbitman, *Just Erotic Romance Reviews*

LooseId®

ISBN 13: 978-1-60737-733-7
DUTY & DEVOTION

Originally released in e-book format in March 2010

Cover Art by Croco Designs
Cover Layout and Design by April Martinez

DISCLAIMER: Many of the acts described in our BDSM/fetish titles can be dangerous. Please do not try any new sexual practice, whether it be fire, rope, or whip play, without the guidance of an experienced practitioner. Neither Loose Id nor its authors will be responsible for any loss, harm, injury or death resulting from use of the information contained in any of its titles.

This book is an original publication of Loose Id. Each individual story herein was previously published in e-book format only by Loose Id and is a work of fiction. Any similarity to actual persons, events or existing locations is entirely coincidental.

Printed in the U.S.A. by
Lightning Source, Inc.
1246 Heil Quaker Blvd
La Vergne TN 37086
www.lightningsource.com

DUTY & DEVOTION

Tere Michaels

Prologue

Queens, New York

"I think this couch just makes me horny."

"How does the bed make you feel?"

Matt blinked. "I think it makes me feel...surprised."

"I want you to come upstairs with me."

"In a minute." Because Matt needed to take care of something first. He put his hand on Evan's chest—scars, heartbeat, muscles—pushed him back enough to reach the fly of his jeans. He held Evan's gaze, and he liked what he saw: still some shyness, still some fear but mostly—this time it was mostly lust.

And maybe something more.

"You break up with me again, I'm going to do something drastic...like move to New Jersey," Matt murmured, pulling open Evan's jeans and reveling in the sound it produced.

"Can't...have that," Evan said, breathless and raw.

"Then don't."

Matt had a tight grip on Evan's cock, and then the talking was over.

* * *

Evan put his T-shirt at the bottom of the kitchen garbage.

He shut off all the lights and headed up the stairs, heading for the bedroom. Matt had already gone up.

Matt in his bedroom.

Evan didn't freak out; he had a single moment of missing Sherri, then gently pushed the thought to the side. Not out of the picture, because she would never ever be completely gone from his mind, his life, but there was room now for both of them.

He put his hand on the doorknob, inhaled, and pushed it open. Matt was standing at the side of the bed, stripped naked and looking slightly confused.

"You, uh…changed the room?"

"Yeah, thought it was time." Evan shut the door, turned the lock.

"I like it."

"Thanks. Sheets are clean," he added, helpful and a little dorky at once.

Matt laughed, shaking his head. Climbed into the bed, punching the pillows like he was settling in for a long winter's nap. Like he was settling in, period.

"Not for long. Get in."

Evan's jeans hit the closet wall in record time.

* * *

Half an hour after happily ever after…

"So…" Evan Cerelli began, staring at the shadowy corners of his bedroom ceiling. From next to him, his—he'd really have to come up with a name that didn't make him cringe—his Matt was coasting toward the edge of sleep, making little moves to find a comfortable spot.

Apparently the "guys sleep after sex" theory was a fifty-fifty split based solely on the occupants of the bed.

"So? I told you, if you try to dump me again, I'm ditching this place for the Midwest."

"You said New Jersey."

"New Jersey is the Midwest."

"No, it's not."

"Everything after the George Washington Bridge is the Midwest," Matt humphed.

"You're not going to New Jersey. Or the actual Midwest."

"Then make sure you don't dump me."

Matt shifted onto his side to give Evan an appraising glare. They'd ridden an emotionally taxing roller coaster over the past few months—falling in love unexpectedly, Evan's injury on the job, the kids, the everything that seemed to propel them into a mess. And he could easily read the aforementioned glare.

"I'm not dumping you. Idiot. The kids would never forgive me," Evan said lightly. I would probably stop breathing, he thought. "I was just going to say…so, where do we go from here?"

"Are you quoting me song lyrics?" The sarcastic tone covered up something which Evan couldn't miss—insecurity. He rolled to face Matt, slipping an arm around his middle.

"Not on purpose. Just trying to get a handle on things."

"You can't relax for like…twenty minutes?" Matt sighed.

"I made sure it was a half hour." Evan smiled.

"Clock watcher." Matt mirrored Evan's position so that they were nearly nose to nose. The heat generation they brewed between them could probably save him thousands on the gas bills for the coming winter.

It also meant they didn't have much time between conversation and the other stuff that made Evan's head spin.

"What do you want to figure out?"

"We're back together, and the kids are…the kids are very happy," Evan began. "I want to make sure we do this right from here on out."

"Okay by me." Matt paused. "And for the record, I really don't know what that means."

"It's just…before you were a friend, and that was fine, comfortable. But now…"

"But now I'm Dad's very special naked-time friend, and that might be a problem?"

"I don't think it's impossible to imagine the kids might get…uncomfortable." Evan didn't get defensive—a fact he was epically proud of—but the worry started to plague him once again.

"I don't want the kids to be freaked out." Evan could feel Matt withdrawing slightly. "You talk to them, see how they want it to go down, and I'm okay with that."

"They love you," Evan said. "I love you. They're great, great kids but I can't take for granted that it'll go smoothly for them."

"Or you." Matt's dark eyes got a little more shadowed. "The neighborhood. Work."

"My boss and my partner know. My kids are happy. No one else's opinion matters."

"Your in-laws…"

Evan groaned. "Ellie knows. Ellie's okay with it."

"That's not…"

"I know that's not what you meant. God, are you trying to keep me awake for the rest of the night?" Evan rolled onto his back, covering his face with his forearm. His former in-laws, Josie and Phil, finding out was his number one nightmare these days, even with the resolve to make things right with Matt and move on with his life.

"This would be a bad time to make a sexually laden remark, right?" Matt deadpanned.

Evan groaned.

"Listen—I know I'm being an asshole about this, but I gotta protect myself." Matt's voice had gone gruff and quiet again. "Maybe down the line we figure out this isn't working, and we walk away. Or maybe we get old together. Either way, I can't do blindsided again."

"Fair enough." Evan uncovered his eyes. "Fair enough."

"We both want what's best for the kids. We both want to be together. The details will work themselves out."

"I don't do seat-of-the-pants very well." Evan laughed. "You might have noticed."

"Fortunately I find your uptight control-freak tendencies attractive."

"Awww, now you're just trying to romance my pants off."

Matt's hand slid under the blanket to the elastic waist of Evan's sleep pants. "Is it working?"

Evan swallowed hard. "Uh...yeah. Actually it is."

* * *

Evan woke up from a deep sleep, his entire body tensing in surprise. He recognized his bedroom (the place where he hadn't slept very much since Sherri's death). He recognized a person sleeping next to him (very much not Sherri and so very much not a dream). For a moment he listened to his rapidly beating heart and the nighttime sounds of the house.

Nothing was amiss.

Matt was snoring lightly into the pillow, pressed side to side with Evan, sound asleep and looking like he belonged there.

After a few moments, Evan sank down deeper under the covers, not breaking the intimate connection between his and Matt's bodies. This was the right decision, he and Matt. It made everything better in a way he hadn't imagined possible after his wife died. The people who mattered most to him were supportive of this—he couldn't worry about his former in-laws or the neighbors or strangers.

He couldn't.

Of course it was easier said than done. Evan knew he lived inside his head too much, only noticed the outside world when there was something to panic about. For so long Sherri had helped him keep those tendencies under control, but without her... Well, it wasn't easy for him to lock the door on those demons.

The shrink helped. His friends helped.

Matt helped more than all of those others put together.

Evan resisted the urge to toss and turn. He wanted a fresh start for them—all of them—but taking the kids out of the neighborhood they'd lived all their lives seemed cruel. He didn't want to make them change schools. And beyond that—could he sell the house he and Sherri had scrimped and saved to buy?

Did they make fresh starts for one's brain? An editing program to take out the crazy thoughts and keep the good stuff.

The house creaked and settled under Evan. He let the clicks of the furnace lull him off to sleep. The details would work themselves out; they would.

They would find a rhythm of their own.

Chapter One

Queens, New York

A Few Months Later

Matt Haight wheeled his overloaded shopping cart through the throng of shoppers in Pathmark; he had a list, a handful of coupons, and the twins to keep an eye on. If he let them run loose, there'd be fifteen boxes of cereal in the cart by the time they hit the checkout.

"Danny, Elizabeth—stay in the same aisle as me, okay?" Matt stopped at a display of shampoo and tried to find the note from Katie (formerly Kathleen, now only answering to Katie—particularly to the hundreds of boys who seemed to call on a regular basis) on his list. She was pretty nice for a teenager with a high IQ, but he knew better than to mess with her beauty routine.

"We're fiiiiiine," Elizabeth sang, skipping over to the cartand standing on the back of it. "We just want to look at the canned pasta."

"Look at it? Really? Or figure a way to smuggle it into the cart?"

"It's just so yummy," she wheedled, flashing her big eyes and dimples.

"It's got enough sodium to stun an elephant." Matt found the exact same shampoo that Katie had written down and put two bottles in his cart. He was three-quarters through the list and almost out of room. Feeding two adult men and three growing children required a flatbed.

Danny appeared at Matt's side looking suspicious; Matt suspected he was trying to smuggle some contraband pasta into the cart. The boy had hit nine and gone into growth-spurt mode. If they weren't feeding him, they were trying to find pants to fit him.

"My God, I'm Susie Homemaker," Matt mumbled, ticking shampoo off his list. "Listen, I might be able to look the other way this once, but you guys have to help me finish this list before I lose it."

"Lose the list?" Elizabeth asked, staring at the paper in his hand.

"Lose his mind," Danny said helpfully, pulling a can of ravioli out from the inside of his sweat jacket. A semishoplift of crap in a can.

"Yes, lose my mind. We have to finish this. We have to run to the drugstore. We have to get Katie at field hockey."

"We have to buy ramen noodles for Miranda to take back to her dorm." Elizabeth found her sister's poor school diet to be an object of fascination and glamour.

"Right." Matt scribbled that onto his list. Two grown men, three growing children and one NYU freshman—next shopping trip he was bringing Teamsters to load the flatbed.

They pushed on into the next aisle; Matt sent Elizabeth in search of yogurt (he had a coupon) and Danny for orange juice (ditto). Matt filled up the last tiny sliver of space in the cart with three gallons of milk and two dozen eggs.

He was rearranging cans of tuna fish and three bags of mixed vegetables when that familiar feeling of "no really, what? This is my life now!" hit him like a hot flash. Lifelong bachelor in a studio apartment last year—taking care of four kids and a semihousehusband the next. Seemingly straight with a string of meaningless sexual relationships for most of his life—living with a guy, in love with a guy, crazy about his kids in the space of fifteen months.

Matt got these moments a few times a week; they weren't regret, they were more like stunned realization. He had no complaints (okay, he really hated food shopping); he had no apprehension (okay, he was a little afraid of PTA meetings). He was in love and content. He'd take a bullet for Miranda, Katie, Danny, and Elizabeth. Hell, he'd change his name to Susie if they needed him to.

Okay, he probably wouldn't make it legal and put it on his driver's license or anything.

"Found it," Danny said, lugging two gallons and looking at the cart speculatively. "This gonna fit?"

"No. Maybe. Okay, we need another cart." He admitted defeat. No amount of reorganization was going to make this happen.

"Can I go get it?" Danny gave a look down the aisle where Elizabeth was still counting out yogurt containers, no doubt picking all her favorites.

"Alone?"

Matt contemplated this. Nine wasn't a baby, and they needed to give Danny some independence, including some time away from Elizabeth, who seemed perfectly content to share a metaphorical womb with her twin forever.

"Okay, but you get the cart and come right back here. No sightseeing, no side trips down the candy aisle. We'll wait right here."

Danny's face lit up; he shoved the cartons at Matt, then sprinted down the dairy aisle, dodging shoppers like a madman.

Matt sighed. He hoped his insurance covered underage cart drivers.

The back pocket of his jeans vibrated, then segued into the theme song from *S.W.A.T* (a daily reminder of Miranda's sarcastic sense of humor). He shifted his hold on the orange juice and grabbed the phone.

"Hey," Matt said, smiling.

"Hey," Evan said on the other end. Matt could hear street noise in the background. "How's it going?"

"Almost finished looting Pathmark, then picking up the prescriptions and then picking up Katie," Matt recited. "When I ask you what you want for dinner tonight, you better say take-out."

Evan sighed. "Actually?"

Matt caught the sigh and followed up with one of his own. "Ahhh, don't need to still have my badge to know the rest of that sentence. Late night, won't be home, eat without me, leftovers in the microwave, I love you and I'm sorry. How'd I do?"

"Unfortunately, perfect. I'm sorry—I really am. Last night this week, I promise."

Matt didn't bother to point out it was Thursday. "Sure, no problem."

Evan didn't say anything for a long time; Matt knew he was being a little bit of an asshole. He knew the pressures of being a detective in New York City—he used to be one. He knew Evan was a workaholic at worst, a devoted cop at best. He understood; it wasn't a problem, but shit, if he didn't want to apologize to every wife or husband of a cop who'd ever gotten bitter or bitchy about the hours and doing it all themselves. "You wanna call later and talk to the kids?" Matt asked, looking down the aisle to where Elizabeth was walking back to him, precariously holding a dozen cups of yogurt.

"Yeah, that's a good idea." The guilt in Evan's voice was heavy. "I'll call around seven."

"Okay. Dinner'll be in the microwave," Matt said with faux cheer and hung up before his guilt and Evan's guilt collided and formed a hole in the time/space continuum.

"You got all blueberry, didn't you?" he asked as Elizabeth kept the stack steady with her chin.

"I'm pretty sure it's the healthiest," she pointed out.

"Odd claim from the worshipper of MSG." Matt looked the other way to see if Danny was coming back with the cart. They were running out of arms.

"It's called balance," she said sweetly.

"Ha, good one." Danny finally turned the corner, and Matt let go of that tiny level of paranoia he had when the kids were out of his sight for too long. "Listen, Dad's working late tonight..."

"Can we get pizza, then?" Elizabeth didn't seem too fazed by the news, but as Danny skidded to a stop next to them, he overheard her question and frowned.

"Dad going to be late?"

"You know, pizza is not code for Dad being late," Matt said, putting the orange juice down and reaching for the cartons from Elizabeth. "Except for in this case, when it is."

"Whatever," Danny mumbled, and while Matt had only been semiparenting under a year, he knew what that meant. And it wasn't good.

"All right, people, let's move out. Danny, you got the second cart, Elizabeth is in charge of coupons, and we're moving on. I think we need butter and cheese and..." He changed the subject as quickly as possible and moved the troops closer to the finish line.

Their last stop was the high school, where Katie had "school hasn't even started yet and there's already" field hockey practice. She sat on the steps waiting for them, all glamorous blonde curls and plaid skirt and knee socks, talking to some boys. Matt resisted the urge to get out and kill said boys preemptively. He knew exactly what they were thinking.

He honked the SUV's horn aggressively.

Katie gave the boys a wave, picked up her bag, and ran to the SUV. Matt barely gave her time to buckle up in the front seat before he took off.

"We're having pizza tonight, and Matt remembered your shampoo," Elizabeth announced from the backseat.

"Dad's working late?" Katie changed the radio station, from Matt's classic rock to people screaming to a thumping bass beat, nabbing a pair of the extra sunglasses off the dashboard and putting them on.

"Yes." Matt frowned. "Who were those boys?"

"Miscreants and troublemakers. I think they're on parole," Katie said blithely, bopping her head to the music.

"Oh right, I forgot to tell you. Those brochures from the convents in the Swiss Alps finally came."

Katie snickered.

* * *

Between the four of them they got the SUV unloaded pretty quickly. Matt turned on the small television in the kitchen for some manly ESPN as he rearranged the fridge and pantry to accommodate all the food. This kitchen was slightly bigger than the one in Evan's old house; it was part of the reason they chose it. Well, that and the facts that the kids could stay in their schools and there were enough bedrooms and two entrances. Which meant that should the "roommate" story be needed, it would seem plausible.

Not that anyone believed that. Matt was amazed at just how quickly their neighbors figured his and Evan's relationship out. If he'd lived next door to them, he wouldn't have noticed unless they were doing it on the front lawn—and Matt happened to be walking by. Apparently in the suburbs—people noticed. At a professional level.

No one said anything to them, but he did note just how few barbecues they were invited to and how many playdates did not happen at their house. He tried not to take it personally. Plus he really didn't want to go to barbecues to make small talk with strangers, or have other people's kids running around.

"I'm ordering the pizza," Katie announced, walking into the kitchen and grabbing the cordless. "By the way, Danny is doing that not talking, sulking thing in the sunroom. Do you want peppers?"

"Okay, okay, and okay." Matt crammed the last box of cereal in the pantry and shoved the door closed. "Any tips on what to say?" Of all the children, Katie was Matt's second-in-command. Calm and levelheaded where her older sister Miranda chose the dramatic, Katie shepherded her younger siblings and Matt through the complicated routine of everyday life. She was also okay with Matt asking her stupid questions—like what to say when tween angst hit the only Cerelli boy child.

Katie shrugged. "I don't know. Mom used to tell me that what Dad did was important, that he was helping people who needed it and stuff like that." She paused thoughtfully. "Then she'd give us all twenty dollars!"

"You're kinda evil," Matt pointed out, almost admiringly. "Order a salad and some broccoli and something for your dad."

"'Kay."

And Matt went off to deal with his least favorite form of almost stepparenting.

* * *

For about twenty minutes, Matt just lounged on the second old couch they'd thrown in the extra room. It housed anything that didn't fit in the rest of the house, which meant two couches, four bookcases, and three assorted tables wedged under the windows plus an old wooden toy chest for a coffee table. Danny remained on the other couch, seemingly engrossed in his DSi. Matt looked at the ceiling, pondered repainting, and then finally cleared his throat. He wanted to get this over with before the food got there.

"So…"

"What?" Danny looked up at Matt, all scowl and averted eyes. Matt didn't take it personally. Apparently nine was the new thirteen.

"Listen, I know you're pissed about your dad working," Matt began, drumming his fingers on the obnoxious rose pattern of the upholstery.

Danny snorted, his fingers never stopping work on the buttons of his handheld game.

"Well, am I wrong?"

"Whatever."

"His job is important."

"Right."

"He'd rather be home."

"Uh-huh."

Matt sighed. "I know you know all of this, and it doesn't matter anyway because it sucks. Period. You don't care about his job—you want him home. I get that. You want me to give you twenty dollars, and we'll call this little talk over?"

That made Danny look up. "Twenty bucks? What do I have to do?"

"Not be all upset and scarred for life because your dad is working late?"

A ghost of a smile made a guest appearance on the corner of Danny's face. "Do I have to sign a paper or something?"

"No, just don't set fires or end up in juvie."

"Deal."

Matt dug into his pocket for his wallet as Danny shook his head. "I'll remind you later."

"Thanks; I gotta go to the ATM." Matt rolled off the couch. "Hey, good talk."

Danny snickered, still shaking his head.

All in all, Matt thought that went well.

Chapter Two

New York City

Detective Evan Cerelli checked his watch for the tenth time in a span of about five minutes. He knew this was important, he knew he shouldn't be so irritated, but shit—he was.

The stakeout of a suspected underground gambling club was rookie work, and he was irritated that a high-profile mayoral election was pushing it to be the problem of senior detectives. He looked through the binoculars, saw nothing—yet again—and sighed noisily.

"You're like a restless five-year-old tonight. I should have brought coloring books," yawned Helena Abbott, Evan's friend and partner, who sat in the driver's seat, occupying herself with a bridal magazine. "Anything?"

"No. Nothing. Why are we doing this again?"

"Because our boss told us to. Because his boss told him to. Because the mayor wants a big bust for the headlines during the elections and cracking down on illegal gambling is PR safe. These headlines need to imply that we're doing our job, but not scare people. Illegal gambling bad—but not scary." She clucked her tongue as she glanced over at him. "Are you new?"

Evan grumbled as he slouched in the uncomfortable passenger seat.

"Everything okay at home?"

"It's fine. The kids just didn't sound too happy when I talked to them." Evan resisted the urge to stomp his feet.

"And Matt?"

"Matt understands. He was a cop."

"Now he's a househusband. I'm betting it's different." Helena held up an opened page under the dim dome light. "What do you think about these shoes?"

"Huh?" Evan squinted. "They're shoes."

"You're a lousy gay person, can I just tell you that?" Helena gave him a glaring look of affection. "Listen, why don't you call Matt, and I'll pretend I can't hear you talking dirty to him."

Evan's face heated up, even as he tried to form the words protesting the "gay" label but came up with nothing. Labels made him nervous, even as he struggled with his own vocabulary on the matter. "Helena, remember that line we talked about?"

"No." She flipped through a few more pages. "My mother is threatening to pick out my dress, Evan. We need to stop her! She's gone hog wild with these wedding plans."

"It's an exciting event for her. You should be understanding." Evan was glad to get the subject off Matt in general. He was mired deep in too many thoughts right now, and he didn't want Helena accidentally (or on purpose) poking him with a stick.

"Well what about me? I am a part of this, remember." She muttered to herself, then tossed the magazine in the backseat. "I realize it's not every day a person gets married, but she needs to chill."

"How's the groom handling things?"

"He hides. The coward." Helena gave her short black hair a quick look in the mirror, fluffing out imaginary things which Evan assumed needed to be gone. Her hair looked the same when she was done.

"The man is a decorated police officer, Evan. Why won't he stand up to her?"

"Because Vic is a smart man?" Evan offered. The upcoming marriage of Helena's mother, Serena Abbott, and their captain, Vic Wolkowski, was at once joyous and mind-blowing. Helena was going to briefly be the stepdaughter of their boss, though his retirement was already in the works, much to Helena's relief. How awkward would morning meetings be with your stepdad?

"Humph. I'm not wearing periwinkle. I don't care if she thinks I'll look like Liz Taylor," Helena mumbled, reaching over for the binoculars. "Still nothing. Oh my God, this is ridiculous."

The ridiculous waste of time—and the wedding talk—lasted another three hours. Evan parked his car in the garage and checked the dashboard clock.

It was 12:07 a.m.

Cursing under his breath, he stepped out of the car, grabbed his briefcase, and headed through the garage into the mudroom off the darkened kitchen. He could smell the remnants of dinner and hear the rumble of the television set—but no kids, no family noise. He'd missed another evening with his kids.

The house was different, but the reality was the same. During all those years with his late wife Sherri, he'd experienced this moment over and over. She'd held down the fort—ran the house, raised the children, made a happy loving home for all of them. After she died, he tried to do that, tried to make the same sort of place for their four children, but that didn't work so well.

More and more he was realizing that Matt saved them all from Evan's fumbling attempts to keep it all together. More and more he was realizing that things falling into place meant Evan had failed as a father—lover? boyfriend? He still hadn't hit upon a term that worked—and someone else picked up his slack.

Matt was the one who did the food shopping and made sure everyone got where they needed to on time. He helped with homework; he broke up arguments over the remote and the last cookie and the bathroom.

Evan just floated in and out when he had the time, like his time in the house was a guest appearance. He knew the kids went to Matt with their problems, big and small. Even Miranda, the eldest and least enthused about her father's choice of partners, spent more time on the phone with Matt than Evan.

The guilt ate up at his stomach like an angry ulcer.

He knew Matt was up waiting for him, but he didn't call out, not just yet. His coat was hung up in the mudroom, shoes under the bench. (Was that new? He didn't remember it.) He plugged his BlackBerry in, then dragged his feet into the kitchen.

Dinner was, indeed, in the microwave. Evan pressed one minute and waited for the noise to pull Matt into the kitchen. But even after the annoying tone that signaled his lasagna was warm, Matt still didn't appear.

Evan took his dinner, silverware, and a beer into the living room, following the sounds of voices. But what he presumed was the television was actually Matt chatting away on his cell phone.

Pausing, Evan waited to catch enough of the conversation to guess who it was. It didn't take long or much skill; their East Coast friends would all be asleep by now. The only person Matt talked to regularly who'd be awake right now was Jim Shea.

Evan swallowed a scowl.

He'd never been the jealous type, more because he married the first person he loved than because of any superior character trait. And yes, he understood he and Matt were technically broken up when Matt and some cop from Seattle named Jim hooked up for one night. He understood their (albeit strange) subsequent friendship.

Okay, he tried to understand their subsequent friendship. He felt entirely out of sync with the idea of "ex-lovers," being as he didn't have one. He had a dead wife and Matt—nothing else to compare his current situation to. Nothing else to incorporate into this annoyed feeling of having someone else intimately know Matt. Sometimes the "intimate" part bothered the most; he had way too many questions about what they'd done and what it was like and how it felt—and not from an erotic "let's talk dirty" point of view either. He wanted to know that Jim was lousy in bed and Matt never wished he was sleeping with someone far more experienced. Far more—free.

Matt was sprawled on the couch in his sweats and a tight T-shirt. Staying home meant he was busy, but there was also plenty of time for running and the gym while the kids were in school. Evan was pretty sure he'd never looked better. And he was laughing, relaxed, and clearly amused by whatever Jim was saying from the other side of the country. Evan thought he looked good and happy, and it wasn't him making that happen and that felt shitty.

He was now officially the jealous type.

"So seriously—Hawaii until you're bored of it? Color me envious," Matt was saying. He must've realized that Evan was standing there staring at him, because he turned his head and grinned.

"Hey," he mouthed, moving his feet so Evan could sit down.

"So listen, Evan's finally home." Matt made a face as Evan settled onto the sofa and laid his dinner on the coffee table. "Thanks for keepin' me company. I'll talk to you in a few days—keep me updated okay? All right, man, later."

And with that the call was over. Evan flipped the top off his beer and drank so he could avoid his need to be in a conversation a little bit longer.

"Hey," Matt said again, tossing his cell phone onto the coffee table. He leaned over for a kiss, his hand sliding over Evan's neck. Evan could feel a wave of heat from Matt's body, feel the purposeful press of his palm.

It aroused him. And it made him connect his lover's reaction to the phone call and that—that stupid jealousy clamped down on the moment.

"Hey." Evan returned the kiss quickly, keeping his body forward and not turning toward Matt for more. "Thanks for waiting up—and dinner."

"Katie picked." Matt's voice was neutral as he leaned back on the couch. "How'd it go?"

"Big fat nothing. Which makes for interesting report writing, let me tell you." Evan got his fork, picked up the plate and started eating—more avoidance than actual hunger at this point.

"Uh-huh. Ask me about my exciting day as househusband," Matt deadpanned even as Evan winced inside. "On a less lighthearted note… Danny had some issues tonight."

"Again?" Evan put the plate back down with a heavy sigh.

Matt shrugged. "He's going through puberty. He's the only male child in the house. His dad's boyfriend is the go-to guy on a daily basis, and yeah, I'm the coolest human on earth, but still. He needs to spend a little one-on-one with you."

Evan knew that Matt wasn't saying any of this to make him feel guilty. He wasn't giving him shit for being gone so many nights lately, but it didn't matter. A defensive wave rose up with the guilt.

"He has to understand..."

"He's *nine*. He doesn't understand anything except sports trivia, video games, and how to open the refrigerator." Matt got up and headed for the kitchen. "Why don't you hang with him on Saturday. I'll take the girls into the city to harass Miranda."

Evan rubbed his socks against the carpet until sparks pricked his soles. Picking a ridiculous fight because he felt guilty was asinine. He missed Matt like crazy—he should be making up and making out instead of making an ass of himself.

Deep in self-recrimination, he didn't hear Matt come back—until the bottle of cold water whacked him in the head.

"No more beer for you. You have to get up in six hours," Matt said, settling back down.

"Yes, dear." Evan drank the water, studied the bottle in his hands. "Saturday—sounds like a good idea. We'll go play ball or something, meet you guys later, and have dinner."

"Deal." Matt picked up the remote and switched on the television; his night-owl ways didn't change, even with an "early-rising" family now.

"Staying up?"

Matt shrugged. "I guess." He gave Evan a glance. "Unless you want to do something else."

"That's a line? Seriously?"

"I have to use lines now? We share a mortgage, dude. Get upstairs, take a shower, and come to bed naked. Jesus."

For the first time since he got home, Evan smiled.

Chapter Three

The weekend activities got things back onto an even keel; Evan hung out with Danny at the park and the batting cages, Matt took the girls into the city to drop off foodstuffs at Miranda's dorm and go shopping (aka, Matt handing out small amounts of cash and standing on the street out front reading sports news on his phone). They met at the end of the day for a rousing meal in Little Italy, where the gnomelike waiters fussed over the children and murmured behind Evan and Matt's backs.

Matt didn't care. He mentioned the NYPD a few times in conversation while they were refilling water glasses and supported that with a glare as he laid his arm on the back of his boyfriend's chair.

They gave them free desserts. Matt was pleased. Pleased until they reached the street and he realized Evan didn't find the whole thing amusing.

So Matt got annoyed with Evan's annoyance. Who cared if the waiters knew they were a couple?

Then they went home, settled the kids, and swapped blowjobs.

The usual process these days.

* * *

Matt had a fairly consistent romantic history with women; the ones that lasted past a pick-up and one night followed the same path—get together hot and heavy, have a lot of sex, don't talk, fight, break up. For a good thirty-plus years, that worked well. He could pinpoint the moments in the relationship with things were going well (i.e., fucking like bunnies) and then bad (i.e., screaming fights in front of a restaurant, in a cab, in his apartment, in her apartment). Things with Evan were different, and not because he was a man. Not *just* because he was a man.

Evan didn't scream or throw things at Matt's head. He didn't do passive-aggressive, which Matt might be qualified as a professional reader of, thanks to his mother. Evan wore a mantle of guilt, a cloak of stress, and a few faces of love and want, switching around and depending on the day of the week and the mood of his children.

So Matt learned the signs, knew from Evan's tone or the set of his shoulders what today would bring. Sometimes it was easy—he could placate him with space or food or sex. When Matt's needs lined up with those, it was perfect.

Sometimes it was perplexing. Frustrating. Matt found it easier to manage puberty and teendom and the drop-off line at the middle school than Evan's moods. Sometimes he felt like—Jesus, things were pretty good and why not just appreciate it? Why not just eat some dinner, hang with the kids, watch a game, fuck around, and go to sleep? Why wasn't that enough of a life?

Then Matt felt guilty and shit for minimizing Evan's problems and worried it would lead to the same feelings that had broken them up before. That led to being fearful, to watching every step, every move Evan made to see if the hammer was going to slam down once again.

That made him guilty and angry.

Which made Evan jumpy.

The cycle was never-ending.

* * *

"So I'm going to take the kids for the long weekend if that's okay," Ellie said as she hung out, elbows down on the kitchen counter. "You guys didn't have anything planned did you?"

Matt and Evan were double-teaming dinner—Matt going in and out to the grill on the back deck and Evan roasting potatoes and onions on the stovetop. Matt paused in mid-walk and checked the almighty center-of-everything calendar on the side of the fridge.

"Nothing on the calendar. Evan?"

Evan turned around, and Matt saw the weird expression crossing his face. He shuttered an inner sigh and went out to commune with the steaks.

When he came back in, Evan was in the fridge, and his late wife's sister was smiling.

"So I take it you got the kids for the long weekend?" Matt said, putting the empty platter in the sink.

"Yes." The petite woman clapped her hands together. Evan's former sister-in-law had been a big supporter of theirs, particularly helpful since Sherri and Ellie's parents were not—as might be expected—thrilled that their grandchildren were now living in a home with their father and his boyfriend. There were occasional threats during angry phone calls, but Ellie could be counted on to calm her parents down—mostly by suggesting they had no money for a lawyer and no chance of getting the children so unless they wanted to never see their grandchildren again, shut up.

Then she moved in with her boyfriend, who was African American, and completed the living hell that was her parents' lives.

Matt occasionally considered feeling bad for them.

"Walt is taking us to Woodstock. His family has a cabin up there, so I thought we could do some hiking and maybe attend a concert."

"Niiiice." Matt gave Evan a sideways look; his boyfriend still wasn't fully involved in the conversation. "Is there room for me in the van?"

Ellie laughed it off and sipped her iced tea.

A few minutes later, Matt was back on the deck with the long fork, poking steaks and drinking a Heineken. A nice late summer night, sun setting over the rows of brick houses, occasional trees blotting the orange glow. Suburbia at its best. He heard the sliding door open and didn't turn around; one of the kids would have loudly announced their presence. The silence meant it was Evan.

"You got a problem with the kids going away? I mean, Ellie and Walt are as trustworthy as you get."

Evan leaned against the fence and signed.

"Of course I trust Ellie and Walt. The kids'll have a great time. Elizabeth might already be packing."

"Then what's the big deal?"

"I don't know!"

Matt heard the frustration and counted to twenty. Slowly.

"Sure you do. You're pissed because someone else thought to take your kids somewhere cool."

"That's not true."

"Of course it is. You get pissed because I'm home and taking care of shit. You get pissed because Ellie knew it was Labor Day weekend and you didn't." Matt swore he wasn't picking a fight—at least in his mind—but shit, if he hadn't suddenly arrived at a wall with no side route of avoidance.

Evan sputtered for a second, but he didn't storm off and he didn't immediately deny anything Matt had said.

Matt poked the steak. It sizzled at him.

"How did I not know there was a long weekend coming up?"

Matt considered this. There were several answers. He felt the best one was, "You didn't have to." It wasn't posed as a question.

"What?"

"You didn't have to. If Ellie didn't come up with something, I would have. Do you have off? Did you ask?" Matt chuckled despite the lack of levity under the setting sun.

"I've been busy."

Matt finally turned to face his boyfriend, catching the tight, chiseled features and military haircut, the neat-as-a-pin clothes even as they were "relaxing."

"Babe, you're always busy. You're always working, and that's cool—I get that. I used to be you." He laughed again, moving the finished steaks to the platter. "But you can't do that and expect shit to get done and then be pissed about it."

"I should be able to do more…" Evan's voice was soft. He moved off the fence and into Matt's personal space, and that melted whatever pissiness might be working up in his soul.

"You're fine and all, but you're not Superman."

"You gave up school…"

"I went to school to find out what I wanted to do with the rest of my life. Turns out I want to chase filthy-minded boys away from Katie and feed this battalion of humans you created."

Evan made a frustrated sound, his hands balled into fists. Matt punctuated his next words with the long fork, feeling ballsy as all get-out. "And you know? I get that that freaks you out, that I'm doing what Sherri did." Saying her name aloud felt bold. "But hey, here's an idea—appreciate it, get over it or change some shit if you don't like it. But give me some credit, okay? This isn't all about you."

He got the platter and his beer and very purposefully walked into the kitchen.

Goddamn, that went well. Okay, maybe Evan was thinking about punching him or changing the locks. But for Matt, the screaming avoider, that was epic. He almost wanted to call his friend Liz the headshrinker and point out how awesomely mature that just went.

"Hey, dinner's ready," he called, waiting for the stampede of feet. Ellie was setting the table with Elizabeth's help.

"Where's Daddy?"

"Shutting off the grill. He'll be right in," Matt said smoothly, throwing his empty into the recycling and grabbing another. "Ellie, you want something more grown-up than lemonade or Diet Coke?"

"Can you open the bottle of wine I brought?" she called.

"Ohhh, classy. What, did you think we only had beer or something?"

"Do you only have beer?"

"Yes."

Matt opened the cabinet door.

"Uhh…"

"A juice glass is fine. At least tell me there's a corkscrew," Ellie said.

"Yeah, it came with the bottle opener."

* * *

Dinner was nice. Evan joined them, quiet at first, then warming up. The kids were jazzed for a trip with Ellie and Walt, who had no children and a lot of spare income, and that meant lots of treats. They discussed the supplies needed for a three-hour drive, staying in a cabin for three days, and the ride back; apparently this involved a lot of chips, canned pasta, and bottles of soda.

Matt glared at Elizabeth who dissolved into snickers as Ellie promised as much canned pasta as they wanted.

"Just 'cause it's a vacation," Matt said, mock stern as he gestured toward the little girl with his fork.

"They'll eat healthy, I promise," Ellie backtracked, but from her expression, Matt knew she'd cave. Probably before they left the city limits. These kids were that good, with the big eyes and sweet smiles and conning ways. Adults were putty in their hands.

The conversation went on, louder and louder until Matt found himself watching Katie, Danny, and Elizabeth compete for their Aunt Ellie's attention. He forgot sometimes their lack of a female figure; teachers were one thing, but these kids had been raised almost entirely by Sherri as Evan worked those crazy detective hours. To go from that to testosterone heaven couldn't have been easy.

He found himself glancing over at Evan, sitting at his side but off in his own world.

"Hey, we should do something for the long weekend," he murmured. "Go away, just the two of us."

"I probably…"

Matt smelled "have to work" as clear as the lingering charcoal from outside. He just nodded and looked back toward the kids.

"I probably have to talk to Vic, find out the schedule. Maybe not the whole three days but at least two," Evan's voice found Matt, low and tense and tinged with something desperate.

Now Matt felt guilty for playing the Sherri card outside.

"Listen..."

"I'll take care of all of it, okay? Just leave it to me."

Matt wanted to apologize but didn't. Something told him it would just make things worse for Evan.

Chapter Four

Evan waved at the kids from the front door as Walt pulled the Expedition he'd rented out of the driveway. They were overpacked and stocked with enough food for the apocalypse, all smiles and blown kisses as they disappeared from sight.

He didn't let it bother him that they'd be so far away. That he'd failed to think of something fun for their last long weekend of summer—his and Matt's spat on the deck that night was so spot-on he could still feel the arrow in the middle of the bull's-eye. At least he'd salvaged something for him and Matt; the small house on the beach in Montauk was ridiculously expensive but worth it. Evan wanted to say thank you and I'm sorry and a couple of other things it made him blush to think about.

Evan hadn't expected to be making all the same mistakes again. He didn't expect after his wife's death to fall in love again, let alone to fall in love with another man.

He'd almost fucked it up. Almost pissed it all away in a swoop of fear, and that still haunted him, even as Matt almost seamlessly became part of their lives. The kids loved him. They didn't just accept him, they demanded him as part of their lives. Evan had no excuses.

So of course, after all that dumb luck, he was working steadily on screwing it up.

When Sherri died so tragically, so suddenly over two years ago, all Evan could think of was how he'd failed her as a husband. How he depended on her too much, how he left her holding the bag one too many times. How much did he want that time back, to apologize or to make it up to her? That wasn't going to happen with her—but he would be damned if he repeated the same mistakes with Matt.

Back in the house, Evan spied the two suitcases near the front door. Upstairs he could hear the shower going. He absently reached into his pocket to check his messages, then threw the phone on the couch.

"Seriously, Evan," he mumbled, kicking off his sneakers as he marched upstairs.

Man on a mission.

By the time he reached the second-floor master bedroom Evan was naked—embarrassingly naked and semihard and shivering a little from both states of being as he put his hand on the doorknob.

Matt was singing. Or more like humming loudly with the occasionally remembered word thrown in.

Evan's heart thumped, and his dick got a little more interested.

He pushed into the room before he lost his nerve—ridiculous as it might seem. Not usually the aggressor, not usually the one that made the first move. But this vacation was the start of a new resolution, one where Evan remembered how tenuous life could be and how not to take his boyfriend for granted.

If anyone in the world knew how life changed on a dime without warning or preamble, Evan did. And he didn't want to ruin his relationship with Matt making the same old mistakes.

The steam level indicated Matt was fully enjoying the water tank and the absence of anyone flushing the toilet. Evan stepped over a pile of towels and Matt's sweatpants, his hand pausing and wavering over the folds of the shower curtain.

"I see your shadow," Matt called over the pulse of the water.

"Those razor-sharp cop instincts still exist."

"Also? I've seen *Psycho* like forty times." His boyfriend pulled the curtain back, soapy and smiling. "You have a license for that lethal weapon?" He gave Evan's dick a pointed look.

"That's a line?"

"I told you—no more lines." And with that Matt erased Evan's foot-dragging seduction and reached for him. "No more courting. You're stuck with me."

Evan ducked into the shower, pushing Matt a step back and stealing the still-hot spray. He tipped his head back, rubbing his hands over his chest and arms in a way he knew Matt appreciated.

Appreciative enough to trace the same patterns with Matt's own hand, stepping under the water to close the distance between them.

"This is a surprise," Matt murmured, pressing his mouth against Evan's pulse point, licking up under his ear. Evan shivered as he wound his arms around Matt's broad shoulders.

"Kickoff to vacation," Evan said, pushing them out of the spray to lean his lover against the tiled wall. "Celebrate the quiet."

"I like it." Matt's dick rubbed against Evan's stomach. "Makes me look forward to what you have planned for the rest of the weekend."

Evan's body blushed and burned as he rocked his hips against Matt's. They'd gone only so far in the past year, both of them exploring all the possibilities but not quite ready for the "final frontier."

Matt wanted it.

Evan feared it.

And then underneath, he thought about it entirely too much to deny that he wanted it too.

There was a porn DVD hidden in the garage. He'd watched it a few too many times, alone, which made it a dirty secret in his mind, something so utterly insane that he knew Matt would strain a muscle laughing at him when the truth came out.

"I have a lot planned," Evan said boldly, pulling Matt's mouth from his neck and burying his tongue down his throat to stop the conversation.

The kiss made everything better; Evan didn't have to say the words, but he could express the want with his mouth, his tongue making pointed stabs against Matt's until they were both mimicking the unnamed need with frantic mouths and urgent hips.

Matt pulled away, his eyes dark and needy. For a split second Evan almost demanded it now, asked for and begged for it, but his knees didn't hold him up long enough to give in. He dropped down, porcelain hard and unforgiving against his knees. He didn't spend too much time on that; he was too busy opening his mouth and pulling the hard red length of Matt's dick against the back of his throat.

He was good at this. Almost too good for a guy with two sex partners, ever. Where Matt could draw it out and leave him begging and cursing, Evan was quick and dirty.

Matt loved it. Loved it and praised him and stroked the short coarse hair on his scalp and gasped and pushed, and Evan ate it up. Sucked it down. Turned himself inside out as he tried to take his lover deeper and make the sounds turn even more harsh and desperate…

It felt like a need, like a drug. He choked a little, felt the water from the shower splattering against the side of his head, but he didn't stop. Didn't even pause. Just sucked and pressed his hands into Matt's hipbones and trailed them down to the inside of his thighs and then back around to tightly grasp his ass.

And that was the key. No need to do more. Just the hint of it, the fantasy he knew Matt had (had whispered in his ear many nights, mouth quiet and frantic, hand on Evan's dick) and Matt's voice went shaky, and Evan knew the end was near.

He didn't pull away.

He should find that shameful or dirty maybe, how easily it came to him. How much it turned him on when that first tiny jerk against his tongue came, how he sucked harder and took it all down his throat, let it flood his mouth, and drank it down.

Dirty little secret—Evan had a few. Matt knew most of them and loved them and loved him.

It was a relief.

And a relief to Matt as he slid down to the bottom of the shower, his hands all over Evan even as he panted through the aftershocks.

"Showers make you really horny—I'm so happy we're going to the beach," Matt muttered, pulling Evan close for a kiss—all tongue and sloppy and distracting because Evan barely noticed when Matt's warm wet hand closed over his dick. "Can't wait to see what those waves do to you."

"Already told you…a lot planned," Evan wheezed, leaning forward on Matt's body, letting him take some of his weight.

"Surfing? Fishing?" Matt gave Evan's dick a wicked twist, down at the base. Evan's body twitched in anticipation.

"Fuck." It came out a moan, and Evan dropped his head against Matt's shoulder, shoving his entire body to find some sort of relief.

"Yeah," and after that Matt apparently had nothing but that ridiculously tight grip and the thrusting of his shoulders and hips, and Evan couldn't think of anything else to say.

Except "ohgodplease" when he came obscenely hard against Matt's thigh.

A quick, cold rinse later, Matt was drying off and eyeing Evan in a bemused sort of way. Evan's shy uptight self got out of the shower—leaving the inner slut behind apparently—and he wrapped a towel around his waist.

Matt rolled his eyes.

"Puritan," he muttered as he walked into the bedroom. Naked.

Evan had nothing to retort, nothing at all.

Matt was in cargo shorts and a T-shirt when Evan was done cleaning up the bathroom. His dark hair curled down around his neck, falling into a flop over his eyes.

"You need a haircut," Evan pointed out and dropped the towel long enough to pull on some boxers.

"Going on vacation, don't need one." He lay back on the bed with a happy sigh. "Might not shave either."

"You're a wild man." Evan put on shorts and an ironed polo shirt—then quickly changed into an NYPD T-shirt that had seen better days before Matt noticed his inability to "dress down."

"I will, however, be taking lots and lots of showers," Matt smirked, sitting and standing in a quick motion. He stalked over to Evan with a gleam in his eye.

"Yeah, I got that."

"I wonder what would happen if we were naked in a waterfall…"

"You watching cable porn-on-demand again?"

Matt didn't look guilty. He didn't hide his wants or desires. Ever. "Maybe."

Evan leaned back against the dresser and couldn't help himself—he smiled. It was next to impossible to do anything but when Matt gave him that look.

"I'm a little nervous what you have packed." That was only half true. He was a little nervous and desperately curious. A weekend away without the kids would be an opportunity for Matt to break out the whips and chains…

"What I have packed? What about you?"

"Me?" Evan flashed on the DVD in the garage. The rental had electronic equipment. They could watch it, they could…imitate it.

Matt snickered; he was clearly teasing, and suddenly Evan felt indignant. Why was it so shocking that he would have whips and chains of his own to pack?

Oh right.

Evan tried to play it cool. He shrugged. "Not showing or telling until we get there."

Matt's eyebrow rose. "Oh really? Now I'm even more eager to get on the road."

"Can you do the lockup and set the alarm? I have a few more things to throw in the car." Evan rocked his hips against Matt's, then dodged his lover's embrace. "Let's get going—we have a long ride ahead."

"Gonna feel even longer!" Matt called at his back as Evan headed downstairs. "How do you feel about handjobs on the highway?"

Evan hurried out of the house. And out to the garage.

Chapter Five

Matt called dibs on driving first, then proceeded to sit in the driveway and honk every five minutes as Evan dicked around in the house. Then the garage. Then the house again. Matt's next plan of action was to start calling every two minutes, but fortunately for the sake of their relationship, Evan came out with the final bag and locked the door, stalking toward the SUV with a fake frown on his face.

"Honking? Really? What was next—phone calls?" Evan got in and buckled up as Matt smirked and backed the minivan out of the driveway.

"Lighten up, baby; we're on vacation." Their first official vacation together, really; the kids were gone, they were out of the house and actually going somewhere. Matt was a little giddy.

"I'm going to bitch about your speeding the entire way there," Evan said drily, putting on his sunglasses and fiddling with the radio until he found something that the kids hadn't preprogrammed.

Classic rock. Matt turned it up a bit to show his approval.

"Eh, bitch away. If we get pulled over, you're flashing your badge."

"Left it home."

Matt navigated through the busy streets of their neighborhood, careful to watch for packs of skating/biking/running kids.

"Lies. You barely shower without that thing."

"Left it home. Told Helena to only call in cases of emergency and that didn't mean wedding complaints."

"Ha. I really don't envy you in the middle of all that."

"The question is actually—how did I end up in the middle? I'm a friend, just a friend."

"You're the best man!"

"That means I take Vic out for... Wait, he's my boss and a recovering alcoholic. What the hell do I do with him for the bachelor party?"

"Club soda and an exciting night of mini-golf?"

"Not helping."

"Yeah, I'm really not even trying here."

* * *

Everyone and their uncle and five of their closest friends were driving out to the island for this last hurrah of a long summer. Matt didn't feel like rushing so he escaped the populated roads and did side and back excursions, enjoying the sun and the breeze as they got farther out. The trees got shorter, the vista flattened, the smell of sea air hinted, and suddenly they were seeing signs for Montauk.

"Almost there," Matt said quietly as he flicked on his turn signal and gave Evan a poke in the ribs. He'd conked out at least two hours ago, snoring and everything.

"Whuh?" Evan sat up and glanced at his watch. "Shit, I was out for a while. You should have woken me up—I could have helped with the driving.

"I did fine. Took the scenic route." He gestured toward the exit on the expressway. "Ten minutes at the most and you'll be unpacking the van…"

"Oh yeah? By myself?"

"I did do all the driving."

* * *

The house wasn't anything special, nothing that would ever appear in any magazine that wasn't titled *At Least It's By The Water*. Matt guessed it was a sixties do-it-yourself kit that happened to be plopped yards from a clean expanse of Long Island shoreline.

He surveyed the kitchen, more sniffing for mold than actually kicking the tires on the oven. It wasn't like they were going to use it.

"It's not the Hilton," Evan said from the doorway, doing his own slightly frowning version of a survey. Wood-paneled walls and red plaid furniture scattered over clean but yellowing linoleum floors was clearly not reflected in the price tag if Matt could judge anything by Evan's face.

And he always could.

"Nope, it's not, which means we can sleep naked and not worry about the maids coming in to empty the wastebaskets."

Matt slapped the faux marble of the small island that separated the living room from the kitchen and tipped his head toward the narrow hallway beyond them. "C'mon—if there's a bed and a toilet, we're gold."

Evan dropped their suitcases near the couch and followed cautiously, like maybe he should have brought his gun just in case some hippies jumped out and tried to make them try pot brownies.

"I didn't bring anything to clean this place with," Evan began, but Matt sighed, grabbed his hand, and headed for the two flimsy doors in front of them.

"We live with teenagers and two nine-year-olds. There hasn't been a germ invented we haven't seen yet."

"Just saying…"

"Blah, blah, blah." Matt elbowed the doors open and discovered a grayish white tiled bathroom, with the wished-for toilet, a sink, and stall shower. A little on the small side, Matt thought, bemused and ever-so-slightly disappointed. He couldn't deny the correlation between his boyfriend's lack of inhibitions and water running.

"Smells like bleach," Evan said, sniffing as Matt yanked him into the second room. A pleasant surprise awaited them; the simple blue-painted walls and starched white curtains on the windows framed a queen-size four-poster bed covered with a green blanket. One dresser, two electronic sconces, and an alarm clock on the windowsill, and that was the entire room. It looked like heaven.

And it didn't smell.

"Hey, this is nice," Evan said begrudgingly, circling past Matt to walk into the room. "Best room in the house."

"As it should be." Matt slid his hands onto Evan's shoulders and squeezed. It was half horny beast talking and half boyfriend who just wanted to relax, dammit. Both of those halves were incredibly pleased with how interested Evan seemed in the bed.

Finding himself attracted to a man was a (mind-altering) hiccup, but it certainly didn't stop the freight train that was Matt's libido. Having sex with one person for this long also seemed to have no effect on what Matt wanted and when he wanted it.

His hands stroked up to trace the tense lines of Evan's shoulders and jawline. Slowly, his lover's body started to loosen and sway back toward him. Matt took advantage of the momentary loss of control and guided Evan against him; their height difference was mere inches, and somehow that translated into the perfect fit of Matt's hard-on against Evan's back.

He soaked up Evan's gentle sighs. He wound his hands down the front of Evan's shirt and fisted the material to bring it up just enough to brush against the warm flesh above his waistband.

Slow seduction.

Matt's mouth against the back of Evan's neck, the way their bodies fit together. The rhythmic shift of their bodies, the give-and-take. Their position—Matt cradling Evan's back against his front—was the start of oh-so-many of his fantasies for the past few months. All of them ended the same way, and he'd be a lying jerk if he pretended that this weekend wasn't the perfect time to bring his fantasies full circle.

"Did we lock the truck?"

"Hmmm? Shut up, stop thinking," Matt groused, sucking hard enough at the spot of flesh behind his boyfriend's ear to stop conversation entirely. If Evan could form full sentences, he was doing something very wrong.

"God." Evan tried to turn around, but Matt tightened his grip, slid one hand under his shirt to keep their bodies pressed together. The slight struggle of his boyfriend kicked off something in Matt's brain that seemed to bloom directly from his lizard brain. Slow, slow, slow, he kept thinking, even as he rocked his aching hard-on against Evan's ass.

"Let me." Two words applied directly to Evan's ear, complete with an exploratory tongue. The resulting hip-bucking response told Matt to stay the course.

"W-what?" Maybe Evan was asking for specifics, and Matt didn't want to disappoint.

"No one here," he murmured, rocking his hips—and Evan's body—as he whispered. "No one outside that door, no one demanding our attention." His hand rubbed circles over Evan's trim stomach, teasing the warm skin under his waistband.

"Ohhh." Evan's shaky exhale was ridiculously hot. Matt skipped slow for a moment, trailing his fingers down to tug at the zipper of his lover's shorts. Evan flailed for a second, but Matt didn't stop. He didn't stop until he flicked the buttons open and lowered the zipper all the way, the fabric gapping to give him plenty of freedom to move.

"Come on, let's get naked." Matt laughed quietly. He moved to pull Evan's T-shirt off.

"We should—" Evan started, but Matt cut him off.

"We should get naked and christen the bed," Matt said. He let Evan turn to face him, completely in love with the shocked expression of want and lust on his face. "I want you so fucking bad," he whispered as he leaned in for a kiss.

Evan moaned an answer into his mouth, one he didn't need articulated words to decipher. He tangled his heads into Matt's hair, pulling their bodies together frantically. Matt sucked on his boyfriend's tongue in enthusiastic response.

The kiss lasted until Matt's constricted dick insisted on getting involved; he pulled back slightly.

"Unzip me," he muttered urgently, half-lidded eyes on Evan's damp mouth.

Evan's hands didn't hesitate, divesting from Matt's hair to attack his fly before the last syllable was out of his mouth.

"Yeah, baby," he said as his shorts were roughly opened and pushed down. The tearing off of clothes happened quickly, separately and together, things flying around the room. Matt felt like he was propelled to their first few times together—frantic and confused and yearning.

But now they each knew what the other liked. Matt knew Evan's insatiable love of blowjobs—giving, receiving, it didn't matter. Evan knew Matt liked rubbing against him until they both came—knew he liked rubbing against Evan's ass while talking ridiculous filth into his ear…that was when it was dark and they were both horny and maybe drunk…

Matt knew what he wanted right now, and yeah, they were going to christen that damn bed right now.

Chapter Six

Evan was naked for the second time that day with the intention of having sex, not something that usually occurred. He was naked in the sunlight, the flimsy curtains not curtailing the warm late-summer sun streaming through the windows. He was hard—ridiculously, painfully so—panting and feeling awkward about where to put his hands but knowing exactly where he wanted to put his mouth.

And there was Matt, just as naked, no questioning or worries written on his face. Every molecule of him was saying the same thing, every flick of his tongue against his lips told Evan where this was going.

Evan thought about the stupid hidden DVD. He thought about the men on the stupid hidden DVD, with their full mouths and their skillful hands. And he thought about them submitting to each other, the sight of which either repulsed or intrigued him—he hadn't yet decided.

He wanted to be one of those men for Matt. He wanted to make Matt moan and collapse and come. He wished he could be that aggressive "top." He wished he could make a move right now instead of waiting for Matt.

Of course, he didn't have to wait long.

"We're not getting out of this bed the whole goddamn weekend," Matt growled before pulling Evan against him.

The brush of their naked bodies together was still so intense. Evan stifled a groan as Matt attacked the curve of his jaw with his lips and teeth. Thinking of the stupid hidden DVD, Evan rubbed his hands over Matt's toned body, concentrating on the smooth muscles of his back and strong hips and God, his ass. Maybe repulsed was the wrong word. Maybe he was thinking of this all wrong…

Maybe he was thinking and that was the problem.

"Told you I had something planned," he whispered as Matt reached his shoulder.

"Oh yeah? Do share," Matt murmured against his skin, pressing his teeth into Evan's flesh until he saw stars.

"Lay down on the bed."

"Good start, I approve." Matt pulled away, trailing his fingers over Evan's mouth, pushing two in. Evan swayed as his mouth watered. He knew what Matt was thinking. Well yeah—he was going to be surprising today. He was.

"On your stomach," he finished, his face burning as the words croaked out.

Matt looked surprised.

Evan felt emboldened.

"Didn't realize this resort came with a massage," Matt joked. He crawled on the bed and settled on his stomach, careful to position his hard cock under him.

Evan felt a little dizzy. He needed—things—he needed his bag, but right now he was naked and too hard to put on his shorts without permanent injury. He remembered something from the DVD (not so stupid anymore) and took a deep breath.

"Just relax," he whispered, climbing onto the bed between Matt's legs, just slightly open as he lifted up to keep the pressure off his dick.

"Got it," Matt whispered back.

Evan realized he wasn't talking to Matt. Matt was always relaxed. Matt was always falling into the next thing with such ease; nothing seemed to faze him.

Taking a deep breath, Evan let his hands trace that familiar pathway again over Matt's body. He had the strangest flash of remembrance—of touching Sherri for the first time, the fear of intimacy and doing it right. They'd done it right and for a lot of years.

He could do this. He could make Matt's pleasure the center of his attention.

The massaging touch of his hands got deeper. Matt moaned under his touch, turning his head against one of the pillows. Evan's skin felt hot and cold, prickling with his own need as Matt's warm, golden flesh yielded for him.

He leaned down, pressing a gentle kiss against Matt's hip bone, tracing the curve of the bone underneath skin with his teeth.

Matt shivered.

Evan followed the path with his tongue, breathing in the taste of salt and the faint tang of soap. He traveled to the small of Matt's back, hairs tickling his tongue. Matt groaned. Loudly. Evan dug his hands into Matt's thighs, stroking and rubbing at Matt's legs until he moved them apart just enough…just enough.

"Uh," Matt started to say, but it was garbled into a moan. "You don't have to…"

They'd never gone quite this far. Faint brushes of fingers. Matt's occasional press of his dick against Evan's, slurring dirty words in his ears until they both forgot just how foreign "that" was. Evan never had the courage to instigate, no matter how good it felt when Matt ventured "there."

He knew without being told that Matt had gone "there" with women. There were allusions; there was the simple expectation that Matt had pretty much done everything one could do that was (mostly) legal with a woman (or two). For all he knew, Matt and Jim—No, he wasn't going there, not at this moment.

Boldly, Evan pressed his palms against Matt's ass, opening him more intimately than they'd ever been before together.

"Want to," he exhaled, leaning forward before he lost his nerve and his need to do this.

Matt stiffened, but he didn't pull away; he just sorted of melted under Evan's fingertips, a perfect expression of trust that welled emotion up in his chest.

Eyes closed, Evan's tongue followed more intimate curves of Matt's body. After you've swallowed a guy's come a few hundred times over a year and a half, was this really the grossest thing ever? Evan thought as he felt the ridges under his tongue. The heat and musky scent distracted ever so slightly so he moved his hands, feeling that familiar connection again.

Matt was moaning. Or rather Matt was cursing and moaning into the pillow. Evan liked that.

Evan liked the way he pressed his tongue deeper—warm, a little wet—and Matt flinched like he was electrocuted with pleasure. That was him in control; that was him doing something to blow Matt's mind.

A little deeper. Maybe curving his tongue. (Because oral sex—he did that. That was this. He'd pleasured a woman for years. No complaints. He could adapt.) Maybe tightening his fingers, pushing Matt a bit more into the bed. Maybe flicking his tongue now, moving away and back again to tease.

Matt's cursing got louder.

Evan trembled when he came up for air, his thumbs replacing his mouth as he kept the pressure up against Matt's sensitive opening.

"You don't..." Matt huffed, but Evan didn't let him finish. He pressed his thumbs deeper, and Matt nearly came off the bed in a restless twitch.

"Want to," Evan whispered, and he wasn't lying. He really wasn't.

They still didn't have what they needed for more, so Evan leaned down again, his tongue joining fingers as Matt pushed back.

Pushed back. Evan was so hard and desperate himself he leaned against Matt's sweat-dampened calf, in urgent need of flesh to connect to his dick.

"Oh God, baby, yeah, yeah," Matt choked out, and Evan's neck protested, and his tongue burned, and his dick fell into a perfect rhythm against Matt's leg, and it was perfect. Stupidly perfect and as hunger inducing as every time Evan was on his knees.

Matt humped the bed, Evan humped Matt's leg, and in a few seconds/minutes/hours it all came to a ridiculously perfect moment when Matt stiffened under Evan's fingers and tongue, poised in an orgasm that the smell of sent Evan into his own frenzied rub.

And it was done.

Done all over the damn bed and Matt's leg, but Evan wasn't moving from where he was—face against the slick skin of Matt's back, draped under him like a blanket.

"I take back every sarcastic comment I ever made about you being a Puritan," Matt said, his voice gravelly and cracked. He reached back to touch Evan's hand, reassuring and gentle.

Evan took a deep breath. "Wait'll you see the whips and chains I hid in the cooler."

* * *

There wasn't actually bondage gear in the cooler, but there were steaks. After a shower and about a gallon of water each (Evan brushed his teeth after they unloaded the SUV—yeah, he was bursting with sexual pride at the hazy satisfied look on Matt's face, but he was still Evan), they found the '60s-era grill on the beach side of the house and filled it with charcoal. They didn't discuss what happened in the bedroom earlier, but Matt couldn't stop grinning or brushing his hands over Evan whenever they passed.

"Just you wait for my turn," Matt said, low and intimate against Evan's ear as he turned the steaks over.

Evan looked at the steak, then turned his head infinitesimally to see if anyone was on the beach. Watching them.

"What? There's no one around," Matt sighed, pulling his hands off Evan with obvious reluctance.

"I'm just—I'd like us to have some privacy." Evan relaxed his face and turned to his lover. "Don't need kids or people gawking…"

"You know, I happen to think you're gorgeous and I'm no slouch, but I'm guessing no one is real interested in two middle-aged guys kissing in a backyard." Matt shrugged, but he backed off. Evan knew he didn't agree with his "hands-off" policy in public, but he didn't push the issue. Much.

"Dinner's ready," Evan sighed. "Let's eat inside, okay?" A compromise because Evan would keep one hand on his fork and one hand on Matt—make him forget this minor bump.

Evan suggested eating in the living room. He found the baseball game and turned it on, grabbing Matt a beer before he could even ask. The steaks were perfect, there were sides he brought from home—even a pretty sickeningly sweet cherry pie for dessert. No leftovers from the microwave for him, no "being in charge of dinner" for Matt.

Vacation for both of them.

Evan settled next to Matt on the couch; when he moved over to give him some room, Evan followed.

"You're fine, stay right there," Evan said, reaching for his fork and knife.

Matt gave him a strange look. "What have you done with Evan?"

"I left him in Queens," he answered honestly, carving into his steak. "I can't promise new Evan is going twenty-four seven, but, uh—I wanted this to be a good weekend."

"So far, I highly approve," Matt said, raising his beer in salute.

"Sorry about outside." Evan waved his fork. "I just—I don't know. I get weirded out by people seeing us together like—intimately."

"I really wasn't trying to fuck you against the grill." Matt shrugged. He looked at the television. "I just don't get the big deal. Unless you're worried about gay bashing or something. But I'm pretty sure we could defend ourselves against that sort of shit."

Evan hadn't even thought about violence; well, there was something else to add to his pile of worries. His concerns were based on what people might think.

He said it out loud without considering what the reason was.

Matt looked genuinely shocked.

"What people might think? There's something so tragic about *ew, gay guys kissing* being thought by a stranger? That's their drama, not ours."

"We're not..." Evan started to say, but Matt cut him off.

"We're not gay? Is that what you were going to say?"

"Yeah, I guess. I mean—we never were. I never was, you weren't—we're just…"

"We're just two guys who sleep together every night and say I love you, and I'm helping raise your four kids? What are you calling that?" Matt's voice raised to a pitch that sounded like a fight was imminent. Silverware clattered against the plate.

"Why does there have to be a label?" Evan dropped his own silverware and stood up, hands rubbing against his shorts. "Seriously—why do we have to say we're gay or straight or anything else? It's our lives. I thought you didn't care what strangers thought!"

"I don't care what strangers think. Fuck 'em. I care about my friends and your kids and you. Specifically and most importantly—you. I care what you think."

"I love you, and I'm not going anywhere." Evan gestured toward the bedroom. "Do you think I take that lightly? Do you think I am raising my kids with you without thinking it over about a thousand times? Labels don't change anything."

"No, they don't. You're right." Matt's voice lowered. He clasped his hands and looked at the floor. "Labels don't matter. But being ashamed does."

"What? I'm not ashamed of anything. I'm just a private person." Evan felt panic bubble up into his chest. "The people who matter know, in both our lives."

"Yeah. So why can't the rest of the world know?" Matt shook his head. "Fuck, this is stupid." He laughed without humor. "I don't know why I'm hung up on this."

"I'm not ashamed. I'm not." Evan sighed. This was exactly what he was trying to avoid. "I love you."

"I love you too." Matt seemed to shake off the bit of melancholy off and gestured back at his plate and Evan's. "Sorry—just... Let's finish eating."

"Okay." Evan didn't know what else to say, and Matt seemed done with it—and God, he wanted not to have this conversation for another second. There was no easy answer with his emotions on this one.

They sat and ate in silence. Evan pressed up against Matt, eating with one hand as the other brushed his arm, his thigh. It wasn't teasing, though—it was reassurance for both of them.

A few hours later, the game was over and the pie was done. Fireflies, crickets, and mosquitoes banged against the screens; moths danced against the sconces outside the front door.

"Tomorrow we'll go down to the beach," Matt said as he flipped channels to the local news. "Supposed to be hot."

"We can swim." Evan lay against Matt's side, their heads sharing a fringed throw pillow against the lumpy back of the couch. No further intense conversations to be had and the amorous mood had cooled enough for Evan to feel bereft.

He needed to stoke the fire.

"I think you made me a promise before," he murmured, watching the temperatures for the rest of the holiday weekend CGI'd across the screen as a cartoon sun wearing shades.

"Hmmm? I'll wash the dishes tomorrow," Matt replied, putting his bare feet up on the coffee table.

"No—not what I meant." Evan turned his body, exploring the strong muscles of Matt's neck. "It's your turn."

Matt's body responded before he could formulate an answer; he clicked off the television and threw the remote aside.

"Right, that's true," he said, sitting up to face Evan—leaving him resting against the back of the couch. "Not sure I can top your, uh—surprise attack earlier."

Evan tried not to preen. "Well, you know. Do your best," he said casually. "No pressure or anything."

"I'll see what I can do."

Matt leaned in a bit closer, his breath warm against Evan's face. Evan closed his eyes halfway, waiting for the kiss, but Matt didn't make contact. He just kept breathing deeply as he moved, teasing Evan with anticipation.

"What?" Matt murmured.

"What?" Evan shifted on the couch, hard and needy, moving restlessly under Matt's dark stare.

"You can't sit still."

"You're being a…a cock-tease," Evan snapped, and Matt laughed against Evan's ear.

"Sounds like a good idea."

Matt didn't do slow and gentle now, no "let's take our time" seduction. His hands were on the waistband of Evan's shorts; then his hands were in Evan's shorts, yanking down the zipper and pulling his dick out through the opening in his underwear.

Evan's head fell back against the couch, his fingers curling into Matt's too-long, so soft hair.

Keeping the "cock-tease" theme, Matt exhaled a warm stream of air onto Evan's skin, the curve of his cock. Evan shivered, tightening the grasp of his fingers.

"Come on," Evan panted as Matt flicked his tongue against the head of his cock.

"Mmmm no."

Evan made a sound of frustration that melted into a moan when the tongue he longed for made contact—against his stomach muscles. He kicked at Matt a bit, trying to maneuver him down, but they were equally matched in strength if not size; he couldn't move Matt off his legs, and Matt couldn't get him to settle.

"Maybe I should flip you over," Matt murmured, his hands dancing over the skin of Evan's inner arm, tracing the dark ink whirls of his tattoo. "Maybe I should tie you to the bed."

The air sucked right out of the room for Evan. His dick pulsed against Matt's cheek, and Matt laughed, dark and knowing.

"Oh yeah? That your secret kink, baby? I can do that." Matt didn't finish the statement, didn't elaborate, but Evan could imagine several scenarios that involved Matt and his police-issue handcuffs and none of them while he was on duty.

"No," Evan huffed, struggling to get Matt off his legs. When Matt did move, Evan wasn't free—no, Matt had taken advantage of his lack of attention and pulled him down onto his back. Now he was flat under Matt's strong body, hands trapped over his head, Matt's hands like Vise-Grips on his wrists.

Evan opened his mouth to say something, but Matt wasn't giving him the chance to protest. Because Evan knew, even as he tried to tell himself this wasn't what he wanted—even as Matt's mouth swooped down and pulled the last bit of air from his lungs—that they both knew exactly how badly he wanted this.

Matt's shorts were rough and grating against Evan's sensitive dick. Every few grinds of their bodies, the zipper metal would graze him. Evan's back arched every time, and Matt took notice. Too much notice, because suddenly Evan's wrists were free—and Matt's hands were on his hips. Moving him, jerking his legs apart as far as the material would allow and then more of the grinding and pressing, and God, Evan's dick was against his stomach and the cloth-covered bulge of Matt's was against his balls…

His hands free, Evan shoved against Matt's shoulders, his head falling back as their mouths tore apart. His head slammed against the couch cushion, Matt over him and still moving.

“Fuck,” Matt was whispering, over and over. Evan could only reach up and hold onto the arm of the sofa, words gone and need taken over.

“Need…” Matt pulled away, and Evan cursed in frustration. He looked up at Matt, who was shaking his head. “Hold on, baby,” he muttered.

His shirt went first, then he pulled his shorts off roughly, kicking them aside. He hovered over Evan, yanking his shorts off before coming back to rest against Evan again.

But the connection of flesh Evan was waiting for didn't happen. Because it was a new angle, a different way for their bodies to fit. The head of Matt's cock brushed against the over sensitized flesh of his ball, then—lower.

Evan groaned, shaking his head. "Can't... Don't have... Wait..." he sputtered, but Matt wasn't listening. And he wasn't pushing any further. Just gentle brushes of soft damp skin against the hidden recesses of Evan's body.

His cock pulsed again, and this time Matt didn't leave him hanging. He felt that large warm hand tighten around his flesh as the pressure against his ass became rhythmic.

It was too much. Too much like the visual fantasy of the past few months, too much like the porn he'd been secretly watching. He could imagine Matt pushing into him, and it was utterly terrifying, even as every stroke of his lover's hand brought him closer to completion.

When he looked up, all Evan could see was Matt's face in utter ecstasy. His eyes weren't focused on Evan, he was staring down between them where their bodies were so intimately touching, and then it wasn't the touch or pull of his palm that made Evan's entire body jerk and spasm. It was the expression of hunger on Matt's face that sent Evan over the edge.

Chapter Seven

Matt watched Evan come and groaned deep in his chest. He had one hand on Evan's wet cock and one hand pressing his thigh up, and God, the head of his dick was just right there against Evan and if he just pushed a little…

Evan whined, and Matt controlled his impulse even as he felt his orgasm tipping point roaring up.

"Okay, baby, okay," he rasped, letting go of Evan as he lowered himself onto his boyfriend's body. His dick fell into the crease of where Evan's leg met his torso, and it was enough to rut against until he came.

"Uh, move," Evan wheezed from under him as Matt rejoined the land of the living. He felt the sweat and come sticking them together in the humidity of the rental house and imagined Evan might be feeling like a squashed bug beneath him.

"Hang on." Matt leveraged himself up on spaghetti arms, dropping himself onto the sisal carpeting with a hiss.

Evan sat up, his expression confused and satisfied at once. He looked down at Matt on the floor and offered his hand.

"That rug is gonna leave marks."

"Mmmm...rug burns. Sexy," Matt said as he grabbed Evan's hand and sat up. "You gonna kiss it and make it better?"

Evan's eyebrows went up. "Right now?"

"Are you under the impression we're done?"

"We're not?"

"Oh hell no. Get into the bedroom."

Matt expected an argument, but Evan didn't protest. He got up, wobbling just a little, and stepped over Matt—who enjoyed the view and made appreciative sounds.

"You haven't been taking Viagra or anything, have you?" Evan asked as he headed for the bathroom.

"No, but you seem to have the same effect as a little blue pill." Matt heaved himself off the floor and followed, licking his lips in anticipation.

"I'm...flattered." Evan was standing at the door, still naked and striped with come, and Matt growled as he closed the space between them to cup Evan's face in his hands.

"You're gorgeous. I want you so fucking bad," Matt murmured, bringing their mouths together.

"You've had me. Several times," Evan said when they broke apart for air. "Not tired?"

"Just getting started." Matt grinned. "Still my turn, right?"

Evan blinked. "If this is the part where the actual whips and chains come out, we're gonna have to have a talk."

"Eh, not really a prop guy." Matt reached down for Evan's hand and yanked him into the bedroom. "But I did bring a few supplies."

Evan snapped on the weak bedroom lights, leaving them shadowy and shaded in the center of the room.

"Like?"

"Like what we'll need for—you know." Matt tried not to lick his lips, but it was impossible. He'd been wanting this for so damn long it was starting to verge on an obsession. And now he had very clear evidence that Evan was seriously into the idea. Which made this the absolutely perfect time.

"Uh, yeah." Evan took a deep breath and stepped back, glancing around the room as if the lube and condoms were going to leap out and yell surprise. "So—do you want to…to go first?"

Matt paused, trying to reconcile conversation brain with lizard let's fuck brain. "First—as in being on top?"

Evan made a face, then looked down as if suddenly realizing he was naked and wearing the evidence of their little escapade on the couch. "Yeah, well—I thought you'd rather be—the other thing."

"The bottom." Matt felt the stirrings in his groin start to wilt a bit. "You thought I'd rather be…"

"Well, I've never done it."

"Uh, yeah, me neither." Matt watched as Evan walked past him and into the bathroom.

"Oh." Evan's voice came from across the small hall.

"When did you think I did, if I wasn't with you?" Matt asked, Twilight Zoned right out of the mood.

Evan came out of the bathroom and reached back to turn out the light. "You know—when you and… When we broke up."

Matt's brain click-click-clicked into place, and he watched Evan walk back into the bedroom, now clean and pulled together, hardly the debauched sexy guy who was there three minutes ago.

"Do you really want to go there now?" Matt asked as Evan sat on the edge of the bed.

Those clear blue eyes looked up at him, cool and shuttered. "I just thought you and he…"

"What? Fucked? I'd just met the guy. I've been sleeping with you for over a year, and we haven't done it. How does that make sense?" Matt was incredulous.

"Well, Jim is gay, isn't he?"

"Yeaaaaah." Matt was starting to feel like he needed to be wearing clothing for this conversation.

"So that's why I assumed—"

Matt raised his hand. "First off, I don't think it's like the law—you're gay, so you take it up the ass."

Evan flinched.

"Or that you even have to fuck someone to make it…" Matt dug his hands into his hair and resisted the urge to pull. "If you wanted to know what Jim and I did, you could have asked at a time other than right now."

"It's relevant."

"Relevant? You can't use that word when we're about to fuck. You just can't. You also can't bring up other people we've slept with while I'm naked. It's just weird."

Evan was so calm and collected on the bed that Matt felt like a hairy beast. He stalked over to the duffels and dug around until he found a pair of boxers, then stepped into them angrily.

"I'm sorry. I just—I don't know why you made the assumption I'd want to be on the—bottom." Evan seemed to struggled with the word.

"Because when we were messing around you seemed into it." Matt gestured toward the living room.

"And earlier today you were pretty into what I was doing, so, you know, not a slam dunk." Evan sighed and reached over for the blanket, wrapping it over his legs.

Matt simmered. "True. Okay, that's true. I shouldn't have assumed."

"Fine."

"Fine."

Matt kicked a tuft of worn carpet with his bare foot.

"So do you want to—I mean, you want to, right? I'm not imagining you're into it?"

Evan cleared his throat. "No, you're not wrong about that." His eyes never raised from the rug. "But I don't know that I'm ready to be—the one it happens to, okay?"

"Okay." Matt looked over at his shaving kit where the lube and condoms were waiting. "So you want me to go first?"

Evan finally looked up. There was something in his eyes, hesitant but yearning, that sold Matt a bit more on the idea. If Evan wanted this, if they both wanted it—why not? "Yeah. I do."

Matt nodded, then walked over to the dresser to unzip his leather kit. He pulled out the tabs of condoms and the lube and tossed them onto the bed; they bounced once and came to rest against Evan's blanketed thigh.

"Okay," he said, courage mounting and waning as much as his dick, which couldn't decided if it was nervous or excited about the prospect.

Evan didn't say anything; he reached out and took the lube and condoms in hand, staring at them for a long quiet moment before looking up at Matt. With his free hand he tossed the blanket off his lap.

"Come here," he said softly.

Matt had done a lot of things with a lot of women over his lifetime. Crazy things, kinky things. The girlfriend who couldn't come unless he called her a slut. The three-night stand (it was a long weekend) who had a vibrator in her purse and redefined the word "insatiable." Thank God for that vibrator, because at a certain point his tongue went numb.

The women in coat closets and maintenance rooms and rooftops and the backseats of cars.

In all the scenarios, it was Matt doing whatever it was that needed to be done. Matt on "top." Matt's dick, leading the charge. But right now, with this man, he was lying again on his stomach, half-limp dick pressing against the covers, not leading anything or anyone anywhere.

He felt cold.

He wished Evan would say something, but for the past few minutes his boyfriend had been entirely too quiet. Evan brushed his hands over Matt's body, gentle and soothing, but it wasn't enough.

Matt needed that edge back, that momentum of excitement and need. Right now he felt like he was waiting passively for something to happen, and that wasn't his style at all.

Evan murmured something, and Matt picked up his head to hear better. The tube of lubricant in his hands, Evan was clearly talking to himself—and reading the instructions.

Matt felt cold and uncomfortable.

"Use as much as you need to," he said, rubbing his palm against the bedspread. "On your fingers."

Evan didn't say anything, but then Matt felt a kiss against his shoulder—then Evan's body spooning behind him, warm and close.

"I…I can't do this, okay?" Evan whispered into Matt's neck. His breath was fever hot, and Matt felt the shiver of his body. "I don't want—I thought I did…"

Matt swallowed. "It's all right—we don't have to do this now."

Evan nodded, pressing closer. Matt could feel he wasn't hard and felt the last stirrings of his own renewed erection fade.

"There's plenty of time. Not like I'm complaining."

"Or me," Evan murmured. He wound his arms around Matt's middle, pulling their bodies together, close and tight. "Not saying never, just not right now."

"Okay." Matt closed his eyes and tried to figure out if he was relieved or disappointed. "It's okay."

"Can we just go to sleep?" Evan asked.

Matt nodded.

They disengaged just long enough to get under the covers. Evan stayed naked, so Matt shimmied out of his boxers and threw them onto the floor. Evan shut the light, reaching for Matt as soon as he rolled back under the blankets.

"I love you," he said fiercely, his fingers tight against Matt's skin.

"I know, I know." Matt soothed him, aligning their bodies together, face-to-face, arms and legs entwined. Nothing sexual at this point but the absolutely most comforting feeling he could create. "I love you too."

He repeated it until they both fell asleep.

When Matt woke up the next morning, he was alone in bed. Not surprising when he rolled over and checked the time. It was nearly eleven.

It was physically impossible for Evan to stay in bed that late.

Matt got up slowly, listening for sounds of Evan in the other rooms. He felt sore, from the strange bed and restless night of sleep. He worried about what the day's conversation would bring, how Evan would be after the incident last night.

He was still conceiving terrible scenarios when the bedroom door opened, and Evan appeared, showered and dressed in shorts and a T-shirt and carrying a mug of coffee.

“Room service?” he said, shy and hesitant at the doorway.

Matt smiled and waved him in. “Did you bring a chocolate for my pillow?”

“No, but I do have coffee here and bagels in the kitchen.”

“Nice.” Matt took the mug and scooted over, giving Evan room to sit down.

“Did you sleep okay?”

“Yeah. Sorry I didn't get up with the sun like you.”

Evan shrugged. “I slept until seven. That's like sleeping in for me. Went down to the beach, took a walk. Got breakfast. Found a nice restaurant for dinner.”

Matt sipped his coffee. “Great.”

“Listen.” Evan toyed with the waistband of his shorts. “I'm sorry about last night. I don't know what happened. I just…couldn't.”

“I told you it was okay.” Matt rested the mug on the bed next to him. “I just thought it was something you were into.”

Evan tensed slightly. “I don't know if it is or it isn't. It's not something I had to consider before.”

“We're not discussing mutual funds, Evan. It's sex.” Matt put the mug back to his mouth to avoid turning this into a fight. It was too early, and it was their goddamn vacation. He didn't want to fight again.

“It's gay sex, Matt. It's not something I had to think about before.”

The way Evan's mouth curled around “gay” made the coffee turn to ash in Matt's mouth.

“Actually it's not 'gay' sex as much a different way of having sex.” Matt shoved the cup onto the nightstand and hauled out of bed. “And again, I don't get the analyzing. We played around, there seemed to be definite interest on both our parts, and so I don't see how suggesting it is a big deal.”

“I'm sorry.” Evan's voice was stressed enough to make Matt stop his angry rifling through the suitcase for clothes and turn around. “I really am. I thought I could do it, and I couldn't.”

“Fine. Whatever. We don't need to do that,” he said, swim shorts and a T-shirt in hand.

“I didn't say never.”

“Right, and I didn't say it was a deal breaker.” Matt stopped at the doorway and gave Evan a backward glance. “I'm gonna change and eat breakfast; then we'll head out to the beach.”

Evan seemed like he had something else to say, but he just nodded. “Sounds good.”

Matt walked into the bathroom and shut the door with a more forceful slam than he intended, wincing as the cheap plywood door rattled on its hinges.

It wasn't a deal breaker, he thought as he looked in the mirror. But more and more he found himself wondering if Evan's inner turmoil about his sexuality was.

* * *

They both tried extra hard for the rest of the weekend. Maybe too hard. Both were accommodating to the extreme—Matt keeping a manly distance from Evan whenever other people were around, Evan with his hands on Matt every second they were alone. It didn't feel forced as much as it felt desperate, and they drove home Monday morning with a sense of disappointment and a ton of sand packed into the SUV.

Chapter Eight

"So okay, here's a question—why do I care if Evan doesn't think we're gay?" Matt asked Liz as he settled down in the "head-shrinking" leather chair of her home office. His good friend and actual professional psychiatrist looked surprised as she swiveled to face him.

"Wow, that's quite a starter to the conversation. I thought this was a social call." Liz's brown eyes widened behind her reading glasses.

"It is a social call. That was a friend question." Matt settled back into the squeaky chair, stretching his legs out as long as they could go. He could nearly reach the Legos her boys had left scattered on the floor.

"It's got shrink undertones." Liz abandoned the paperwork she was futzing around with and leaned back to give Matt her full attention. "I'm also a little leery of the grammar."

"Har har. Now help me."

"Right." She steepled her fingers to her chin, teeth worrying her lower lip. "So Evan doesn't think he's gay or either of you is gay?"

"Both. Mostly him. He says he doesn't like labels." Matt rolled his eyes. "I think he's got this whole shame thing going on, but it's like—what does he think we're doing? Is he secretly creeped out by it?"

"Is he going to try and break things off again?"

Matt thumped his head back against the chair. "Liz, please. Not Dr. Liz."

"You gotta let me blend here, Matt." Liz smiled. "Both the doctor and I know that's where this is coming from. If Evan is so uncomfortable with the perception or concept of being gay, he might end things again, kick you out of his life."

Matt nodded, his face twisting into a scowl. He'd rather face a strung-out junkie with a gun and nothing to lose than spend five minutes contemplating life without Evan or the kids. "Yeah."

"So it makes sense that it would bother you."

"I'm glad I make sense."

"It happens on occasion." She tilted her head at him. "Do you consider yourself gay, Matt?"

"Well, Dr. Liz, I've actually been thinking that over, and yeah—I think so. I mean—technically bisexual since I wasn't faking it with all those women," he said drily. "But if I look at me and Evan, it's…different with him."

"You're in love with him."

"Yeah."

"And you could see yourself in love with another man?"

"Don't want to."

"But you could."

He pondered. He thought about Jim. He thought—yeah, if he had to do it again, he'd probably find himself going wherever it was middle-aged gay guys went to hook up.

"Yeah."

"So you're identifying at this point in your life as gay, and you're concerned with Evan's self-perceptions and how they affect you." Liz leaned over to pat his hand. "You know he has to do the work inside to make his own decisions, right?"

Matt blew out a deep breath. "You mean I can't just yell at him until he stops making me crazy?"

"No."

"That sucks."

"Come on, Haight—you're better than that now. No yelling or picking fights around the issue. You have to confront it head-on."

"I try. He says labels don't matter, and it's no one's business and that's that." Matt toe tapped a small pile of Legos, making them shake and quiver. "Which is true, but it's also not true."

"True."

"Are you this sarcastic with other patients?"

"You mean the ones that pay?"

"I've turned into his wife," Matt added, throwing his mental burdens out one by one. "Or he's trying to turn me into her."

Liz frowned a bit at that. "What do you mean?"

Matt shook his head. Maybe he was wrong, maybe he was going overboard with this. Maybe the whole sex thing during the beach weekend was making him crazier than it should. “I don't know. I feel like I—took her spot. I take care of the kids, I take care of the details and he works, and it's like she never died.”

“I'm guessing that's a bit of an exaggeration. I don't believe Evan mistakes you for Sherri.”

“He'd rather she was here than me.” There. He'd said it. Aloud even.

“Evan didn't get a divorce. His wife died—tragically young. Yes, you're going to feel like a replacement. In some very tangible ways, you are. In other ways you are a unique force in Evan's life.” She paused and made a little “hmmmm” sound in the back of her throat. “Maybe you just want him to recognize that.”

He opened and shut his mouth, teeth clicking audibly.

“I know you know these things. And I know you can connect the dots between them,” she said gently.

Matt moaned as all the pieces of their arguments clicked into place into his head. Being gay meant being different than Sherri, and it was something that was his and his alone with Evan, and there needed to be things about them that weren't just re-creations of Evan's old life. And God, he really hated Liz sometimes.

“I kind of hate you,” he sighed, and Liz clapped her hands.

“Painful truths and eyes opened to inner clarity—that's what I bring to the table, Haight. You knew that, and that's why you came here. Now friend Liz will take you into the kitchen and feed you apple cake with some sympathetic back patting thrown in."

"I like sympathetic back patting."

In Liz's huge kitchen, Matt found his familiar place at her island with coffee and the aforementioned apple cake. She even took sympathy on his hangdog expression and offered whipped cream.

"Evan's jealous of Jim," he announced, licking apple crumbs off his fork.

"One-night-stand Jim?" she asked.

"My friend Jim," he corrected. "Stop making it sound sleazy."

"Oh, sorry." Liz coughed into her hand. "I forgot your delicate sensibilities."

"Just because I used to be a man-whore doesn't mean I can't have delicate sensibilities about some things."

"Point." Liz considered Matt over the top of her mug. "Does Evan bring Jim up a lot?"

"Yes. At ridiculous times—not when I've talked to him on the phone. No, he brings him up when we're..." Matt gestured. "You know."

"Evan brings up Jim in bed?"

"Yesss."

"That makes sense."

"It's gross."

"Jim is his rival in bed. He's not used to that."

"Jim isn't his rival in anything. Jim is some guy I slept with once and who lives three thousand miles away and who I talk to on the phone." Matt could see where this was going, and he was putting his stubborn hat on. Evan had nothing to fear from Jim—nothing.

"Jim is the only other guy you've slept with, which makes you one up on Evan sexually—and when you add on all your other women and compare to Evan's only sexual experience besides you being his wife…" Liz rolled her eyes. "Come on, this is Soap Opera 101 here, Haight."

"I may be a househusband, but I don't watch soaps." Matt sniffed. He reached over and snatched a piece of her cake, chewing defiantly.

"You know, you're really going to have to bring me tougher problems," Liz sighed. "These are softballs being lobbed at me."

"Sorry my pedestrian issues aren't exciting enough for you, Dr. Liz. Maybe you need to get back to forensic work."

"Maybe I will." Liz pushed her plate over to Matt's side of the island. "What about you?"

"What about me?"

"Maybe you need something of your own again—something that isn't taking care of the house and kids."

"So I should get a job?" Matt considered it, but nothing of interest immediately came to mind. He liked being home, liked being around the kids. He liked going to the gym when it wasn't crowded and taking a run through quiet streets, not fighting rush-hour traffic.

"Or a hobby or—something. Something just yours and no one else's. It might help ease your feelings that you're just replacing Sherri."

"Hmmm... Maybe." Matt finished Liz's piece of cake and his coffee.

"That'll be three hundred dollars."

"I'll pay the receptionist on the way out."

* * *

Matt took advantage of his quiet day to putter around before heading home to pick up the kids. He went to the gym after leaving Liz's house and stopped by a bookstore to rifle through the magazine section. The Relationship aisle he passed on the way there almost lured him in, but he kept walking. He doubted anyone had written a book to address his special snowflake problems at the moment.

But when he thought of books, Matt thought about the "joke" books Jim sent last year. *The Gay Kama Sutra*, if he recalled correctly. When he moved in with Evan and the kids, most of his books and non-sentimental items ended up in the sunroom—which is where Matt found himself wandering into when he got home.

It took a few minutes, but under the textbooks and old *Sports Illustrateds* he found the box from Jim and the book, still tucked neatly inside.

They'd not really ever used it. With all Evan's jealousy of Jim, Matt didn't think it a great idea to pull the book out at bedtime and announce where it came from. Hell, the title alone might send Evan fleeing out of the room in sheer horror.

He stared at the cover for a few minutes, thumbed through a few pages. His groin showed some interest—that was a nice mood lifter.

Maybe it was a pipe dream to imagine he and Evan could find this mutual ground, where labels didn't matter but shame wasn't in the equation. Maybe they could find a way to express their sexual desire without all that baggage suddenly throwing itself into the middle of things.

Maybe he should take his own advice and shut up, appreciate what they had instead of wishing there was more. Who cared if Evan considered himself gay? So long as he came home to Matt every night, why did it matter?

Fuck, this love thing was complicated.

* * *

"So dinner? The four of us? Isn't that a little weird?" Matt stirred spaghetti sauce in a bubbling pot on the mess that previously was their stove. The cell was wedged to one ear as Jim's amused laughter answered him.

"Maybe, a little. But why not? I think it'll be fine. We're all adults."

"Hmmm…and I guess you're technically not an ex because you know, been in that situation unintentionally—ex meeting current, and it was ugly. Authorities were nearly called."

"Ha. No, this is just four grown men having a nice dinner and me getting some enjoyment out of an evening of theater."

"Theater?"

"Griffin's friend Daisy is opening in some big Broadway play." Jim sighed. "It's not even a damn musical—that would keep me awake. It's a play."

"That's where they just talk, right?"

"Sadly, yes. But I promised. And Griffin's dad was supposed to come with us, but he's had bronchitis for weeks. I don't think he's joining us."

"I feel like your backup plan. Color me insulted." Matt turned off the stove and opened the oven to check on the store-bought lasagna. His stomach growled in perfect tandem with the smell wafting upwards.

"You're more my opening act."

Matt could hear a riotous amount of noise sneaking through the phone and walked to the fridge. "Where are you? A carnival?"

"Griffin's house. He has eight sisters."

"Holy hell."

"All older. Some are married. Their spouses are here. And their kids. And at least five dogs."

"Is it a party?"

"Oh no, just dinner." Jim sounded bemused. "I'm a little nervous what a party would look like. I think they rent out the Knights of Columbus."

"Nice." Actually it did sound nice, and Jim seemed to be enjoying himself.

"So we on for dinner? This Saturday night—our treat, your choice."

"How can I say no? I hear you retired cops are made of money." Matt was wondering how he was going to convince Evan of this idea when the oven timer went off.

"It's a date, then."

"I'll talk to Evan and give you a call back tomorrow."

"Fantastic. Talk to you later, man."

They said their good-byes; Matt hung up the phone and leaned against the side of the fridge. Was he trying to force an issue here? Was he creating a situation where he and Evan would blow up into tiny pieces, and he'd be proven right—this couldn't last? Matt took a deep breath.

Maybe he was. Maybe he was pushing Evan to get a reaction.

Maybe he didn't care.

Chapter Nine

"So, Jim and his boyfriend are in town," Matt began, and Evan automatically turned around to pretend to be interested in raking leaves out from under the tree.

"Uh-huh," he said noncommitally.

"He wanted to know if they could take us out to dinner."

"Not sure of our schedule."

"This Saturday night."

"The kids..."

"Oh please." Evan turned back at the snappish tone of Matt's voice and decided this was not the moment for some classic passive-aggressive behavior.

"Okay."

"Okay? That was quick."

"Hey, I'm trying not to be a jerk here. If you want to have dinner with some guy you slept with once and his boyfriend—hell, why not?"

"I knew it."

Evan dropped the rake against the tree and kicked it for good measure as Matt stalked toward the house.

"I'm sorry, I'm sorry," he muttered, big strides catching up with Matt as he walked through the sliding glass door into the kitchen. "Matt, I'm sorry, okay? That was a cheap shot."

"You really wanna go over this again? You broke up with me, and I spend one night with one guy who turns out to be part of the reason I'm even here, right now, in domestic *bliss* with your grouchy ass, and you can't spare an evening for dinner? You are a dick."

Evan winced. "Yeah, I'm a dick. A slightly jealous asshole as well."

"Good point." Matt's volume dulled slightly; he jerked open the fridge to take out a beer. And didn't offer Evan one.

"New boyfriend, huh?"

"Yeah. I'm glad for him," Matt said pointedly between drags of his beer. "He's a good person, and he deserves this."

"Vacation?"

"Post-retirement trip. They're traveling. The boyfriend is a writer. They got a friend opening in a play on Broadway, so they're in town. And they called to ask about Saturday night."

"So do I have to wear a tie?"

"Will it make you feel better if you do?"

Evan smiled even if Matt didn't. "Yeah."

"Fine. Wear a vest and one of those pocket hankie things if it'll cut down on the jealous dick factor." Matt's face was serious.

"I won't be an ass to your friend."

"Thank you."

"Really, I won't."

"Fine."

The stand-off didn't feel over. Evan crossed his arms over his chest.

"What?" Evan watched Matt struggling with saying something—or not saying something.

"Why is this such a problem with you? You don't even know Jim, but you act like you hate his guts."

Evan struggled to find a way to express himself that was neither dickish nor jealous, but really, there wasn't much else on his mind. "I guess I just don't understand your friendship."

"Well, not to be an asshole, but you really don't have a lot of experience with this whole ex-lovers and people you've dated and shit like that." Matt sighed and finished off his beer quickly.

Evan winced, but he didn't disagree. "True."

"And I'm not parading a shitload of exes through here. One—that's it, and you know, considering my crappy track record with relationships and general male whoring ways for like, two-plus decades, that's not bad." Matt mumbled a bit to himself, and Evan felt sorry for being a dick about this even if he didn't quite know how to stop.

"Well let's just make a pact this is your only ex paraded around, and we know my closet is clean and there you go," he offered.

Matt sighed. Evan knew the constant bickering was starting to get to the other man; years with Sherri taught Evan that sometimes even the person you loved most got on your last nerve. And that was okay. Natural even.

Matt never had that before. Evan's mood shifted from jealous dick to reassuring lover in a nice move that had him a bit impressed with himself.

"Come on, we're making this into a big deal, and it shouldn't be," Evan said smoothly. He got a quirked-eyebrow look of suspicion from Matt. "Well it shouldn't. On either one of our parts. We'll go to dinner, I'm sure I'll find this Jim a decent if not hideously ugly guy, he and his boyfriend will go to a play and then fly back to the other side of the country, and then we'll come home. It'll be fine."

He managed to cajole a half laugh from Matt and walked over to close the distance between them as quickly as possible. "You should be flattered."

"Oh really?"

"Yeah, because the thought of you with anyone else makes me kinda crazy."

Matt's other eyebrow joined the other in their dubiously surprised expression. "Sexy jealous as opposed to dickhead jealous?"

"Yes.

Matt considered it. "I admit, I like that better."

"Kids aren't home."

"We raked leaves, had a tiff, and now we're gonna sneak upstairs before the kids come home." Matt sighed dramatically as he reached out to grab Evan closer. "We're so suburban."

"What would be less suburban?" Evan pressed Matt back against the fridge, trying to do sexy grinding through layers of fall outerwear—all while not knocking magnetic sports schedules to the floor. It wasn't as easy as one might imagine.

"You, on your knees…right now," Matt drawled seductively. He was more effective slipping his hands under Evan's jacket and pulling his shirt out of his pants.

And yeah, that sounded good. They'd been dancing around each other in the few weeks since they got home from the beach. The bedroom wasn't a dead zone, but both seemed to be holding part of themselves back, as if not wanting to approach that "losing control" line again.

Evan missed the naked passion, the times when Matt just didn't care or stop himself from saying or doing what he wanted. He wanted that back again, even as he spent daily hours worrying over "the next time" and whether or not he could go through with it.

"Being gay" meant a lot of things in Evan's head. It meant wanting to sink down on your knees in front of your boyfriend and unzip his shorts in the middle of the kitchen just so you could feel his dick on your tongue and his hands in your hair. It meant wanting to hear dirty whispers of how good and hot and tight your mouth felt as he pushed his cock to the back of your throat.

It meant getting hard in your pants just from the taste and the smell and feeling of his ass under your hands as you rock him harder and faster until he's gasping for air and you're swallowing and it's so, so good you don't need anything else.

It meant that you did need him to sink down onto the floor over you and pull at your clothes until you were naked and writhing and begging for something—anything…

And for Evan, it meant this terrifying moment when he was so undone by Matt's come on his lips and his own throbbing erection that when Matt rolled him over and pulled down his pants and pushed his tongue into the place he couldn't imagine being the center of his need—he didn't fight it. He didn't protest or push Matt away as he was filled and fucked.

That was the word. It was Matt's mouth and tongue, but he was being fucked and every stab felt indescribably good. And it shouldn't. It shouldn't but it did, and Evan moaned and pounded his hands against the Pergo wood floors in absolute perfect pain.

Matt didn't let him deny it anymore.

Matt held him open and down and took the orgasm right out of him, taking his cock into his hand at the last possible second and sliding from root to tip once—just once—and Evan came with a choked cry against the floor.

Maybe Matt knew the second it was too cold and too strange to be down on the floor. Before Evan could dissolve into self-recrimination, Matt was pulling him back and up, into his arms, letting him lay back in his strong hold.

"Hey, that was fun," Matt whispered against his ear, and Evan huffed out a laugh.

"Floor needs a cleaning," he whispered back.

"Is that a critique of my housekeeping or a compliment on my lovemaking?"

It didn't sound entirely like a joke; Evan's heart thumped and settled—he turned his head a little, enough to look at

Matt's face. "It's a compliment," he said softly. Whatever his hang-ups and fears, he loved Matt deeply. There was no denying that.

"I should hope so," Matt huffed. He shifted back and moaned—not in pleasure. "Old knees, protesting…"

"Right, let's go upstairs." Evan reluctantly moved out of Matt's embrace and stood up, gathering his clothes. They were both naked from the waist down, sweaty and disheveled.

Evan's shame meter blipped slightly, but it got drowned out by the damp aftershocks still stirring through his body. He could deny and deny for the rest of his days, and not a word of it would be true. The way Matt touched him triggered something so deep and needy in his very soul—he felt like a key had been turned inside him, one even stronger than the first time they'd kissed.

Matt wasn't privy to his thoughts, his wonderment. He was heaving himself off the floor, bitching about old age and cold wood floors. He picked his clothes up and looked at Evan, pausing at the expression on his face.

"What?"

Evan shook his head. He couldn't verbalize it, not yet. Not until he came to terms with it.

"Nothing." He smiled, reached for Matt's hand. "Come on. Bare-assed in the kitchen is weird."

The kids came home, and they had a normal night. No one seemed to notice Evan's distraction or catch a clue of his internal monologue.

Why did he like that so much? Why did he want it so much? What did that make him?

The idea that his life with Sherri was a sham, a cover-up to a confused sexuality, made him sad. It made him angry. It made him wonder what would have happened if Sherri hadn't died. Would he still be turned on by her for ten years? Twenty years? Would he one day have woken up and felt like a different person?

Matt, oblivious and sleepy, lay on the sofa, his head pillowed on Evan's thigh. The local news was on, the forecast over, the sports highlights winding down. Domestic bliss. Evan trailed his fingers through Matt's hair, remembering when Sherri used to do the same for him, soothing him as he tried to drift off after a long day.

Who was he? Who was Evan Cerelli, and what the hell did he want and need?

* * *

Friday night, Evan found the book. It was crammed under the nightstand on Matt's side, thumping to the floor when Evan was trying to straighten the mattress out. He picked it up and glanced at the title.

The Gay Kama Sutra.

He turned the first page and the inscription could his eye.

Call him.

Underlined for emphasis.

Then, a little below that:

I recommend pages seventeen, thirty, and forty-one. Stretch first.

A wave of conflicting emotion rolled over him. He knew exactly who this book was from, the only person it could be from.

Call him—Jim sent this book after he and Matt slept together, before Evan and Matt reconnected and got back together. Jim had been encouraging Matt, encouraging him not to give up.

Evan owed him a thank you.

But the other lines—they gave him a lurching feeling in his stomach.

It was probably a joke, but—but he couldn't help feeling intimidated. Jim didn't need a book. He could imagine there had been no fumbling or confusion the night they spent together.

Evan's fingers tightened on the book, and even as he resolved to put it back from where it came, he couldn't help but flip through a few more pages. The illustrations were graphic but tasteful, and Evan paused at more than one, his mouth dry as he brought the book up closer under the light.

His clothes felt tight and constricting. His first instinct was to stick his hand down his pants and relieve the needy urge welling up inside him.

The second thought was to find Matt and crawl into his lap and whisper things in his ear that Evan didn't imagine he'd ever say out loud.

He did neither. Shutting the book, he stashed it back where it was and righted the bed.

He wasn't ready. He just—wasn't.

Chapter Ten

James "Jim to almost everyone else" Shea straightened his tie in the hotel bathroom's mirror. He could make out enough of his visage in the fogged-up reflection to pronounce himself fit to socialize.

"We're going to be late," Jim called to his boyfriend, who was currently attempting to use every drop of hot water in the Marriott's tanks. And possibly all of New York City's.

"Shhhh, I'm relaxing," Griffin's voice called over the hard spray of water.

"Ahhh, so all those weeks in Hawaii followed by being spoiled at your dad's house really did a number on you—we're lucky you haven't broken under the strain."

"You're harshing my buzz, man." The water shut off, and Griffin poked his head out, a comical expression on his face. "Dad's did not have this amazing water pressure."

"You act like we got clean by sitting in the creek and beating ourselves with rocks."

"Kinky. It's always the quiet ones," Griffin said drily. He wrapped himself in a fluffy white towel with a blissful sigh. "I'm from Hollywood, man. I like the luxury."

"Well, put on your fancy-pants suit and shiny shoes—we have good seats for this…play." The word dropped off Jim's lips like a bowling ball crashing into the floor. He was less than thrilled with their plans for the evening, though the consolation for sitting through Griffin's friend's play was seeing his old friend Matt Haight for dinner.

A double date. Him and his boyfriend and the guy he met for a one-night stand and his boyfriend. It was either the setup for a porn movie or a disaster of epic proportions.

"You have to promise not to snore," Griffin said. He dried off and immediately reached for the ever-present products he used to keep his unruly hair out of his eyes. Jim refrained from commenting on the sheer volume of items on the bathroom counter. "I mean it; we're in the front row."

Jim groaned and ducked out of the bathroom. The steam was getting to him.

"Hey, I'm having dinner with some guy you're buds with because you screwed said guy in a bar pick-up scenario. I need leverage and leeway here." Griffin came out of the bathroom massaging gel into the wet wavy mass on his head.

"It was before you," Jim said, uncomfortable.

"Right, I get that. I'm fine with that. Mutual virginity was not a requirement of us." Griffin stopped, hands on his hips, watching Jim with a mixture of humor and love. "It's just…a little weird."

"We're friends—that's not weird."

"One-night stand, e-mails, phone calls. Chummy dinners with current lovers. There's a script here somewhere." Griffin finished with his hair, his eyes squinching up, as if he'd just realized he could barely see Jim without his contacts or glasses.

Jim sighed. "Okay, Hollywood, get dressed. I promise not to snore during Daisy's play; you promise not to take notes during dinner."

Griffin's eyes nearly rolled out of his head. "I promise to behave."

"Cross your heart? I know how you are after your second cocktail."

"I promise not to blow you at the table."

"Good boy." Jim made shooing motions.

"You say that now. I know how you get after your third beer."

Griffin stalked back into the bathroom with a jaunty hip move and a whistle. Jim briefly reconsidered the entire dinner and "play" evening in favor of sex with his ridiculously hot younger boyfriend…but figured he didn't have the romantically suave moves to talk (or blow) Griffin into skipping the play in particular.

Griffin had issues to deal with when it came to his former best friend Daisy Baylor. Jim had some issues as well—mostly how to keep from shaking the famous movie star until her IQ notched up a few dozen points and she realized how much her boneheaded actions nearly ruined Griffin's life.

He was doing this for Griffin and his "closure." He wasn't under any impression that Griffin and Daisy were done with each other—you weren't friends with someone your entire lives to just dump them. At least Griffin wasn't that person. He wouldn't give up on Daisy or their friendship or anything, anyone he loved.

Reason number 104 Jim was stupid crazy about him.

So he'd watch the dumb play and stand around with his lips zipped when Griffin's and Daisy's phone calls went from "once in a while" to "all the damn time" again. He would perhaps quietly mention caution and trust, but he wouldn't be surprised when famous movie star Daisy reentered their lives.

* * *

They took a cab to the restaurant as butterflies danced in Jim's stomach. He was suddenly flashing to that night when he and Matt met and recognized kindred souls—middle-aged guys with a sad sack of no prospects and not much time to change the course of their lives.

Except they both did. Both of them were walking into the restaurant with exactly what they were yearning for that night. Matt had Evan back, and Jim had… Well, Jim had Griffin, who was a surprise and a gift and not the person he was yearning for back then.

Thank God.

"Good Lord, man, I was kidding before. Relax," Griffin muttered, giving his tightly fisted hands a squeeze. "I don't mind this. Hell, I'm curious." His boyfriend's grin glittered under the passing bright lights of midtown, bouncing off his glasses. "He's a dead ringer for me, isn't he?"

"Your twin," Jim said. He let his hand linger on Griffin's, then rested on his knee. "It's eerie."

"I knew it!" Griffin snuggled a little closer, assuring and warm. "You wanted me before you even met me."

"Something like that."

They passed the next few minutes of traffic and congestion in silence before the cab pulled over in front of the restaurant. Jim overpaid the cab driver as Griffin nearly jumped out of the backseat; clearly he was now in anticipation mode.

"Hurry up. We're like five minutes late."

"What happened to being fashionably late?" Jim straightened his tie and smoothed a hand over his nearly non-existent hair.

"That's Hollywood. This is New York City—I think we're supposed to be early."

"Let's go back to Hawaii, where no one needs to be anywhere but the beach."

Griffin gave him a sympathetic look and slid his arm through Jim's. "I can't believe Mr. Workaholic likes retirement so much."

"It's only been a few months. I might get antsy at some point."

"We'll figure out a hobby for you. Like—needlework or painting landscapes." Griffin led the way through the front door of the small bistro they'd selected to meet Matt and Evan at.

"Ha."

"No, really. We'll ask my dad what he likes to do." Griffin smirked as he slid his jacket off. The two men had gotten along so well that he'd constantly joked about being a third wheel.

"Shut up, youngster." Jim took his jacket off and looked for the hostess. She approached with an armful of menus.

"We're meeting someone here. Might be under Haight?"

"They're already here. I'll take you back." She gave them a pleasant but not flirty smile. A quick scan of the bar showed a mixture of couples, mostly same sex. Jim felt comfortable laying his hand on Griffin's back as they followed her to an intimate corner.

Matt Haight and his boyfriend were seated; Matt looked great—comfortable and in great shape, working a black knit sweater with some serious confidence. Jim felt the memories of the two lonely men from last year disappear a bit more from his mind. His boyfriend was neatly put together in a suit and tie, that tightly bound look recognizable to Jim in an instant. All business, always on guard. He didn't look as delighted as Matt when they spotted him and Griffin near the table.

"Hey, hey, look who's here!" Matt stood up and came around the table to give Jim a hug. Jim didn't resist—no matter how tight the boyfriend's lips got. His own boyfriend was already extending his hand for a shake.

"Griffin Drake. Nice to meet you," he said politely as Jim slapped Matt on the back.

"Hell, you look good. Life is agreeing with you," Jim smiled as he appraised Matt up close. He was right—he looked fantastic.

"You too. Nice retirement tan." Matt winked as he gestured to the man at the table. "Jim Shea—Evan Cerelli."

"A pleasure." Jim extended his hand. "I've heard a lot about you."

Evan nodded politely and shook Jim's hand. "Same here." His tone was flat, so Jim ended the handshake quickly for both their sakes.

"Uh, Griffin you've already met. Matt, Griffin, Griffin, Matt."

Griffin smiled sweetly. "Nice to meet you. And you're right—it's like looking into mirror."

Matt looked confused as Jim shook his head.

"Ignore him. His blood sugar is low, and he gets nonsensical when that happens." They sat down as Griffin laughed at his own joke.

"Quick, someone pass the breadbasket before I say something inappropriate." The patient hostess handed the two newcomers their menus and drifted off for quieter confines.

They made general small talk while perusing the menus: the weather, the traffic, a quick overview of Griffin's famous friend the movie star, who was doing a play.

"I'm really excited about it," Jim deadpanned, as Griffin explained the "mermaid and a pirate play poker" symbolism.

"It's going to be excellent," Griffin insisted, kicking Jim under the table.

Matt took a sip of beer, not bothering to hide his smile.

"Darn, sorry to miss it."

"Liar." Jim decided on the steak and snapped his menu shut. "We do have an extra ticket, though—Griffin's dad wasn't feeling well and didn't make the trip down."

"I couldn't ditch Evan, even for metaphorical pirates," Matt said, putting his arm across the back of his boyfriend's chair.

Jim caught the slight tensing, and was confused for a moment, until the waiter announced his presence behind them.

They ordered quickly, drinks and food and the waiter sauntered off. Jim gave Evan another glance, but he didn't seem to have relaxed.

Griffin—as Griffin was wont to do—took the quietness at the table as an invitation to do his very best chatter. Griffin's father claimed as soon as soon as the boy uttered his first words, he made it his goal in life to fill uncomfortable silences.

He told some genuinely funny Hollywood tales and a good one about Jim on catamaran in Hawaii. Jim allowed the entire story to be told—even the part where he lost his swimming trunks.

"It was quite a spectacle," Griffin smiled, giving Matt and Evan an eyebrow waggle. "I was worried we'd get followed home by the gawkers."

Matt laughed heartily. Their drinks hit the second round; Evan stopped drinking, murmuring something about driving later. He didn't say much of anything else.

Food saved them for a while, saved poor Griffin's voice. Jim considered other topics as he cut into his steak. Police work was obvious, but he didn't want Griffin to get bored.

Although technically it was payback in advance for “The Wager” he would be subjected to later. A pirate and a mermaid playing cards? Really? People paid for that shit?

“So, Evan, you're a police officer?” Jim heard Griffin say. His heart swelled a bit; his boyfriend was trying, really trying, to make this evening a success.

“Vice, almost fifteen years,” Evan said quietly, picking at his tuna.

“Wow, cool.” Griffin waited a beat. “You ever do any undercover work?”

“No, not really.” Evan seemed to struggle to say more, a side glance to Matt who was stabbing his pot roast with an annoyed air. “I think I look a little obviously too much like a cop.”

Griffin squinted at him appraisingly. “Yeah, no offense.” He gestured toward Jim. “Like Officer Stud Muffin over here. It radiates off you guys.”

Matt seemed to be amused by the conversation; he pointed to Evan. “When we first started hanging out, we went to this bar. And they knew we were cops without saying a word. I'm convinced it's a secret skill of bartenders.”

“Like that place we met,” Jim said before entirely thinking the statement out. Everyone at the table was aware of how they met and what happened afterward (generally—Jim didn't kiss and tell, even when Griffin begged jokingly for details in bed that morning). And clearly not everyone was comfortable with it.

See: Evan's expression of distaste.

"Uh-huh," Matt said, obviously feeling the temperature drop as well. "Exactly. I wonder if it's something they, uh—teach at bartending school."

"You gotta know who's carrying," Griffin said helpfully. "Or who could be a hero during a robbery. Or who you have to bribe for protection." He even used air quotes.

Jim loved him, so very much.

"All he knows about cops he learned from television."

Griffin sniffed, faux insulted. "Whatever. Everything you learned about everything else you learned from television."

"I don't even know what that means."

"Humph." Griffin went back to his meal, sneaking peeks at Jim and doing a whole "Seriously? The tension!" conversation with his mouth full of pasta. Jim was impressed.

The rest of the meal was awkward chitchat, mostly between Jim and Griffin, with Matt chiming in. Evan excused himself to go to the men's room, Matt said he had to make a phone call, and Griffin kicked back the rest of his third martini after they both walked away.

"Fuck, this is like the most tense dinner date ever!" he whispered, futzing with his hair in a clear nervous gesture. "Evan hates you, by the way."

"Thanks for the update, Scrappy Doo." Jim sighed as he stretched back in his chair. They had at least an hour more to kill before the play, and dessert didn't seem like a good idea at all.

Griffin glanced back toward the back of the restaurant. "By the way, Matt seems very nice. And he looks nothing like me—can I surmise he's more like me in bed?"

Jim sighed. "No, you may not. This is not a comparison or a contest, which is probably what's going through Evan's head. It's a slightly different situation, okay? I mean..." He realized he should have told Griffin this before, but it felt awkward to share too many details. "Evan was married before this. To a woman."

"Should I be, like...offended or shocked by that?"

"No, of course not. But he and Matt never dated men—until they met."

"Ohhhh. So this is a late-in-life thing."

"They're younger than I am, you know."

"Right, late in life." Griffin smiled sweetly.

"Anyway. I think Evan's a little uncomfortable with Matt sleeping with me."

"Because you have a giant, amazing dick and the mere act of sex with you makes Matt yours forever?"

"You're cut off from drinking right now."

Griffin laughed, leaning against Jim. "I love you. I love teasing your grouchy ass."

"Mmmmm, tell me that's a euphemism for something, please."

"We have a play to go to, but afterward, I promise." He tipped his head for a kiss and Jim, as per usual, was unable to resist.

"Ahem," Jim heard Matt say as they pulled apart. Matt and Evan had returned; Matt was smiling, a little sadly, and Evan—Evan was looking around in a slightly frantic way, as if to see what reactions around them were.

There were, of course, no reactions that Jim cared about, but he gave a glance as well. No one seemed moved by their tame kiss to look up from their meals.

"Sorry," Jim said, giving Evan a sympathetic look. Suddenly the discomfort seemed to be a bit clearer.

"Don't be. Just don't get carried away. Don't want Evan to have to arrest you," Matt said lightly. He sat down and shook his empty beer bottle. "Seen the waiter?"

"Yeah, we should get some coffee," Griffin said, though he looked a bit longingly at his martini glass.

"Maybe Irish coffee is a good compromise," Jim offered. He looked around until he caught the eye of their waiter. He hoped he communicated, "Come quickly, please," to get him to hurry.

"Dessert? Coffee?" he asked.

"God, yes—and another round of drinks." Griffin bit his lip a second later. "Let me speak for myself—just me is fine."

"And me," Matt said.

"Hey, ditto." Jim coughed into his hand. "And a pot of coffee." He glanced at his boyfriend. "Chocolate cake?"

"How well you know me." He turned to the waiter. "Two pieces of chocolate cake."

Jim looked at Matt, who looked at Evan, who looked at the waiter. There was a long pause.

"Sounds good. I'll have the same," Evan said finally.

"Nothing for me but the beer." Matt finished off the ordering, and the waiter left. The silence lingered.

"So, Evan"—Griffin leaned on the table, all fake cheer—"thanks for having dinner with us. I know it must be a little awkward."

"Oh God." Jim kicked him under the table so hard his shoe nearly flew off.

Griffin ignored him. "Really. I think it's great that we don't let any of that ruin Jim and Matt's friendship."

Evan's mouth moved, but didn't open; he was flat-out flummoxed.

"I mean—hey, let's face it. We don't come into a relationship without baggage, right? We have all this stuff that comes with us. And you have to deal with it, or whoa—elephant in the room."

"Which I wish would sit on you," Jim murmured. He looked helplessly at Matt.

"I'm just saying, I understand." Griffin rolled his eyes. "I'm being sympathetic."

"You're also being a brat. Sorry."

"Ugh, did you just apologize for me? Jesus Christ, Jim—I'm going to pop you in the jaw when we get outside."

Matt...laughed.

"I like him," he said. Jim noticed he didn't have his arm on the back of Evan's chair, wasn't leaning into his space.

"You want him? He's housebroken."

Griffin was still focused on Evan; they were locked into some sort of staring contest.

"Shut up, like you could live without me."

Jim considered this. "An excellent point."

Griffin settled in, elbows on the table, not blinking.

Evan did the same.

Jim looked around for the waiter.

* * *

"Really? That was just crazy shit," Jim fussed, herding Griffin into a cab after saying good-bye to Matt and Evan—who had headed off toward the parking garage with a cloud of "oh we're gonna fight" gliding over them. "Did you have to get into a pissing match?"

"There was no pissing. There was staring." Griffin gave the address of the theater to the cabby. "And you know what? I get all the other shit, I do. I get he's uncomfortable with you, with me. But did you catch his expression whenever you got too close to me? My grandmother is more tolerant than he is."

"Exaggeration." Jim sighed as he stared out the window. "He's not entirely out, and he's uncomfortable. You should be more tolerant."

"Whatever. It bothered your friend Matt."

"I know. I know."

"That sucks."

Griffin's annoyance segued into a quiet sadness. Jim reached down to squeeze his hand.

"I feel bad for both of them," he said finally.

"Me too."

"You should call Matt tomorrow and see how he is."

"I will."

"And you should—listen, I'm just throwing this out there, but maybe if Evan needs someone to talk to…"

"I thought you correctly deduced he hated me?"

"Okay, so maybe you're not the ideal person for him to speak to—there's always me."

Jim patted Griffin's hand. "I love you, so much, but, uh—you were at the restaurant a few minutes ago, right?"

"It was tense. So what? I've lived in Hollywood for ten years. I can kiss your ass one day and string it up a flagpole the next day. It's an art form."

"You keep talking about my ass—and I have to sit through a whole stupid play. Stop teasing."

Griffin elbowed him. "Tell Matt to tell Evan if he wants to talk…"

"Right, Dr. Phil. I'll mention it."

"Thank you. I'm just saying—make the offer."

"You're a very nice man."

"Thank you."

Jim leaned over and kissed Griffin on the cheek.

Chapter Eleven

"Griffin!"

Jim turned his head as the feminine voice reached his ears. Griffin was chatting it up with the set designer whom he apparently knew from a shoot—honestly Jim wasn't paying attention. He was still trying to estimate the distance from their location in the middle of the lobby to the bar and how fast he could get there and back.

He gave his boyfriend a poke in the side as he gestured over to where Daisy was fighting through the crowd.

Sans arty mermaid costume, Daisy looked like herself—mostly. Jim noticed most of her red hair was gone, styled into a little pixie cut that made her look about half her age and height in one fell swoop. She seemed so tiny as she worked her way through the well-wishers and hangers-on, he fought the urge to sweep through and clear a path.

"Griffin, Jim, hi," she said breathlessly, finally making it into their little circle. "I'm so glad you're here."

For a split second, he worried what Griffin's reaction would be—after all, their everyday contact had been limited for the past few months to brief, awkward phone calls. But then Griffin was moving past him to throw his arms around his childhood best friend, lifting her off the floor with an audible squeak.

"Don't break her. I didn't get enough cash at the ATM to pay for a movie star," Jim said as Griffin whacked a few people in the shins as he gave her a whirl.

Daisy giggled nervously as Griffin set her down.

"So you're glad to see me," she said, a little desperately, and Jim gave another glance toward the bar. Three drinks, he could carry three.

"Yeah." Griffin sniffled as he smiled at her.

Jim decided to wait on the bar, and let his boyfriend lean against him, doing the quiet physical reassurance thing and trying not to glower at the woman who had betrayed her friendship with Griffin.

She clearly didn't expect an affirmative answer from Jim, but she gave him a sidelong peek. He cleared his throat and tried to relax his facial muscles.

"The play was, uh—good. I didn't fall asleep," he offered. Daisy smiled and bit her lip.

"I think that's high praise." Griffin sighed. He was rubbing Daisy's arm, and they both seemed on the verge of weepy hugs.

"It is," Jim said.

Daisy gave a watery laugh. "I really appreciate you both coming, really. I know I can't apologize enough for what I did…"

"Water under the bridge," Griffin said.

"But not entirely forgotten." The words slipped out, and Jim endured the whip-quick look from Griffin. "Forgiven, though. You did your best to fix things, and I appreciate that. You didn't let Ed Kelly down."

He left out the part where she kind of let Griffin—her best friend forever and a day—down, but he didn't think anyone needed the reminder. Daisy's face was pale, her bottom lip was quivering, and Griffin's glare was burning a hole in the side of Jim's neck.

"Thanks, Jim," Daisy murmured, her gaze dropping to the hem of her flowy black dress. "I know I don't deserve your forgiveness."

Two fingers to the neck of his shirt—Jim was starting to get uncomfortable. It's not like she killed someone…jeez.

"We all have to move on," Griffin said, his voice tightly strung. "New day and all that—the play was amazing, Daisy Mae. You were incredible."

The praise perked Daisy up a bit, and Jim resisted the urge to roll his eyes.

"Thanks. Bennet and Shane really deserve most of the praise. It's a brilliant play." She fluttered her eyelashes. "And Lance, of course."

Jim had no idea who any of these people were. He suspected Lance was the guy who played the metaphorical pirate. Truth be told (and he wasn't going to join the praise-a-thon just yet), he'd just about held his own against Daisy—she carried the show. And was probably the only reason Jim hadn't fallen asleep.

"Would you two like to meet Bennet?" Daisy linked her arm into Griffin's, giving him a little tug. "He and Shane are over there." She indicated an area much closer to the bar than they currently were, and Jim found himself nodding enthusiastically.

"Sure, sounds good," he said, answering for Griffin, whose "WTF" expression was probably the highlight of the evening.

They moved through the crowd, with a few mini-stops as Daisy graciously thanked people for their ass kissing.

Two men were huddled together between the bar and an exit door—Jim thought it might be the best seat in the house. Both had that hipster look he was so fondly dismissive of. He girded his loins and waited for the introductions to begin.

"Bennet, darling, come meet my friends," Daisy called, zipping around the tightly knit bar crowd to duck between the two men. The darker of the two—hair, eyes, and eyebrows so black they looked blue—brightened when he saw her, arms opening to pull her close.

"Can I meet them too?" The other man was the opposite end of the spectrum, fair-haired with blue eyes and a killer "aren't I charming?" smile. Jim checked to make sure his wallet was still in his pocket.

"Of course, silly." Daisy had brightened considerably since the rather deep conversation, tucked in Bennet's arms but being handsy with the other man as well.

Weird people.

"Griffin Drake, Jim Shea—this is Bennet Aames and Shane Lowry. Bennet directed the play, and Shane is the writer," she said, complete with gestures.

The men all exchanged handshakes, murmurs of pleased-to-meet-yous. Then Bennet (his hands still on Daisy) smiled broadly at Griffin.

"So you're the infamous Griffin—I'm really delighted to meet you, young man. We have a lot of business to attend to, you and I."

Jim's eyes narrowed. Was this a hit-on sort of thing? Griffin looked a bit starstruck, an expression Jim hadn't really encountered before. Griffin was a screenwriter—why did some play director make him look like he was about to pull out his autograph book?

Griffin gave Daisy a weird look, and she just giggled.

"Your screenplay?" Bennet glanced over at Jim. "I was hoping while you're in New York we can discuss it. Are you here for long?"

"We're sort of on an open timeline," Jim said, casually—deliberately—putting his arm around Griffin, just in case these showbiz types had any funny ideas.

"Excellent—that means Griffin and I can set up a meeting…" He looked hopefully at Griffin, whose expression was starting to brim into something resembling "burst of light."

"Should I be jealous?" Shane asked, all faux innocence and appraising looks.

Jim looked at the bar. So close and yet so far…

"Not at all, unless you've forsaken playwriting for the bright lights of Hollywood," Bennet smiled, an even line of very white teeth blinding them all. He pulled out his iPhone

one-handed, swiping his fingers until he "ah-ha'ed" at the screen.

"Are you free tomorrow for a late lunch? We could meet at my office, if that's all right with you. Then perhaps I can get you all to come to dinner with us."

Griffin was already nodding so Jim joined in.

"Sounds great, thank you." Griffin smiled. He gave Jim a glance for confirmation.

"Perfect." Bennet put the phone back in his jacket pocket and signaled over their heads for someone.

Jim prayed it was a waiter.

"Would you two like to come with us? We're going somewhere more quiet for a cocktail."

"Or ten," Shane added. He seemed to be a part of the "us" package that included Bennet and Daisy. Every sort of 'dar he had was going off; Jim was pretty sure Bennet and Shane were coasting toward gay on the Kinsey scale, slightly sure at least one of them was also sleeping with Daisy, and mildly concerned "cocktails" meant "cocaine."

"This isn't going to be an orgy or anything?" he murmured to Griffin, who elbowed him in the side.

"I'll protect your honor," Griffin whispered back. At least the glaring was over. And maybe the cocktails would mean sex and not violence when they got back to the hotel room.

In a little pack they moved through the crowd—more ass kissing, now with good-byes scattered in—Jim and Bennet were about the same height so they managed to clear the way for Daisy, with Shane and Griffin chatting up at the rear. It was sort of second nature for Jim, scanning the perimeter and analyzing who was around them. All the shiny faces seemed the same. Too much alcohol, too little sleep, trying to impress…

It was almost an afterthought that the man lingering near the doorway caught his eye. He didn't have a drink in his hand or a hip outfit on his slender body. His head was ducked down as if he were trying to avoid eye contact—which was pretty much the last thing anyone else was doing. Jim felt his body go into an alert stage, slowing down as he passed the man, to get a better look.

His hands were deep in his pockets, his gaze averted. But when Daisy passed his position, his head jerked up, and Jim saw glazed eyes and a desperate expression.

He moved quickly, pushing his way between Bennet and the man—but the latter was a split second closer. Faster.

"*Daisy*!" he cried out, throwing himself toward her as she reached the sidewalk, off balance as she shrugged into a short jacket. The stage hand passing it to her went down first, a look of surprise crossing his face as the man bolted in front of Daisy, his hands grabbing for her. "*Daisy*, you have to listen to me!" he screamed.

Bennet froze for a moment, but as Jim stepped forward—hands pushing the man back—he regained his senses and shielded Daisy with his body.

"Get her into the limo," Jim said, his eyes never leaving the crazed man now throwing himself against the solid wall that was the retired cop. Chaos behind him was a dim soundtrack; he just wanted to know this guy wasn't carrying.

"Call the police!" Someone shouted as Jim grabbed the guy's arms, trying to keep him from pulling anything deadly out. The tell-tale bulge of a weapon brushed his hip, and he tensed, throwing twenty years on the force into a quick takedown onto the pavement.

Chapter Twelve

The ride home was not a chatty one; Evan drove with the radio loud and tried to decide if he was more pissed or embarrassed by his behavior. Probably a perfect storm of both. *He* went with the best intentions of being polite and friendly, but at the restaurant he just felt open and exposed, like every single person there could see through his clothes and skin and read his mind. And when they came back to the table—after whispered heated words in the hallway—Evan was slammed by the sight of Jim and Griffin kissing.

Which made him think about Jim kissing Matt, and then everyone in the place seeing it, and his brain took a detour into ugly.

He cleared his throat; he considering speaking but maybe that was like throwing a rock into a war zone and seeing who fired. Matt's head snapped to the side to shoot a dagger into the side of Evan's head.

"You promised," he said simply.

Evan sighed. "I know. I know."

"You're better than that—whatever the fuck that was back there." Matt blew out a frustrated breath, his head turning back away from Evan. "They didn't deserve that."

Evan flinched.

“And you know what? Neither did I.”

The boom lowered. Evan's fingers tightened on the steering wheel.

His BlackBerry buzzed in his pocket. He welcomed the distraction of work as he recognized Helena's number.

“Hey, what's up?”

“Sorry to bug you, but I was out with Chris Callas from Midtown, and she got a call about a disturbance at the Muse Theatre.”

“And…is this something that's going to end up on our desks?” Evan asked, motioning for Matt to lower the radio.

“No—but didn't you say Matt's friend was going to the opening night of the play there? Chris said a retired cop took down someone who went after the actress.”

“Oh. Shit.” Evan glanced at Matt whose attention was drawn to the conversation. “Is everyone okay?”

“I guess so. Ambulance on site, but that's pretty standard.”

“We'll head over there. Thanks for the heads-up.”

“No problem. See you tomorrow.”

Evan hung up and began to pull off on the next exit ramp. “We should head back to the city. There was a problem at the theater where Jim and Griffin were going. Someone went after the actress.”

“Shit.”

“Exactly. And apparently your friend took the guy down.” Matt held onto the dash as Evan pushed the speed limit to get back to midtown. He was glad his badge was in his pocket.

The place was a madhouse when they pulled up. Evan flashed his badge at the cop directing traffic and got a wave-through. They parked on a side street, and Matt was leading the way, clearly forgetting he wasn't still on duty.

They worked their way through the onlookers, cops, and EMTs who were wandering around—not to mention the press throng that seemed to be multiplying by the second.

"Detective Callas?" Evan asked as he showed his badge to a uniform outside the yellow crime-scene tape.

"Yeah, in there." The officer gave Matt a look and smiled. "Haight? That you?"

"Barney? Jesus, they got you on crowd control? Good to know the city is safe," Matt grinned, shaking his hand warmly.

Barney shrugged. "Hey, I might even score an autograph for my son outta this. Not a bad night."

"Everything under control?" Evan asked.

"Yeah. Some guy off his meds went after the actress, and her bodyguard or someone took him down."

"I heard it was a retired cop."

"Guess so. Looks cop. Or military. He disarmed this guy before he got near her. We're just here to keep the press from swarming the place." He shook his head.

"Listen, I know the guy in there—he's a friend. You mind?" Matt gestured toward the building.

"Nah, go ahead." He nodded at Evan as well. "Have a good night, guys."

"Thanks, Barney. Take care."

Evan and Matt ducked under the tape and headed into the theater.

"Do you know everyone?"

"Generally." Matt grinned. They entered the lobby where there were way fewer people—just cops, a few EMTs, and a small crowd of people. Evan recognized Griffin right away.

"They're over there," he motioned to Matt. They closed the space, with Evan spotting Chris Callas amongst them.

"Griffin?" Matt said the younger man's name, and he turned, his face full of shock and drained of color.

"Everything okay?" He nodded to Chris, who had apparently gotten the heads-up from Olivia that they would be there.

"No one was hurt, and the suspect's been transported," Chris said.

"Jim won't go to the hospital," Griffin blurted out. A blond man was standing at his side, nodding to Evan and Matt.

"Just a few bruises and a bloody nose. They just wanted to check him out," he added.

"The EMTs said he should go." Griffin had clearly hit fretting mode, and Evan felt bad for the young man. While this was old hat to Jim and himself and Matt, Griffin had clearly not been around this sort of thing in his life.

"I'm sure Jim knows if he needs medical attention or not," Evan said, falling into detective mode. "The EMTs are probably just being overly cautious."

"See, that's what I said." The blond man smiled at Evan and Matt. "Shane Lowry," he said by way of introduction.

"Detective Evan Cerelli. Matt Haight." Evan turned his attention back to Griffin, laying a hand on his shoulder. "Why don't we go over and talk to Jim. I can probably tell if he should go to the hospital, and we'll convince him, if that's the case."

"Uh, okay, sure. Thanks." Griffin glanced at Shane, then seemed to search the small group for someone else. "Is Daisy okay? I have to go…"

Shane put his hands up. "Go on, see to your boyfriend. Bennet and I got Daisy, and the cops are here. It's all good."

Evan nodded at the young man, sparing a glance at Matt before heading toward the chair in the corner where the EMTs had Jim sitting. The other man had an ice pack to his head and some bloody gauze around his knuckles as the technician took his blood pressure.

The grousing could be heard within a few steps.

"I'm fine, okay? Fine. I can go back to the hotel."

"Jim?" Griffin went to stand next to him, his hand gentle on his shoulder. "Jim, Matt and Evan are here."

Jim looked up, and Evan could see the split lip and bruised cheek as well. "You got the call?"

"My partner was with the lead detective and let me know." He looked at Jim sympathetically. "How bad?"

"We're concerned about a concussion," the EMT started, but Jim waved her off.

"I'm fine. I've been knocked around before, and I don't have a concussion. I'm going to have a headache in the morning, but that's it. I'd like to get the hell out of here." He looked up at Evan, full scowl on his face. "Can you give us a lift?"

Evan looked at the tech who seemed exasperated but not overly insistent. "Sure, we can take you to the hotel. Griffin, are you going to feel okay keeping an eye on Jim? Checking for signs of a concussion?"

Griffin's face turned a lighter shade of white, but he nodded. "Yeah—I can do that."

"Yes, he can do that. Now, I'm leaving." Jim stood up defiantly and quite possibly willed himself to not even sway. Evan was impressed. "I'm keeping your ice pack."

The EMT snapped closed her kit. "Fine. Consider it a gift from the people of New York."

"Fabulous."

Griffin and Evan flanked Jim, walking him over to where Matt was waiting. Evan noticed his boyfriend speaking to a dark-haired man who had protective arms around a petite woman.

"Hey, nice black eye," Matt said as they approached. "You harass the paramedic until she let you go?"

"Yeah, better get me out of here before she changes her mind."

"Oh Jim," the redhead sniffled, coming out from the other man's embrace. "Thank you. You saved my life."

Jim didn't seem in the mood for the conversation; Evan held him up while Griffin reached over to kiss the woman's cheek.

"You okay, Daisy Mae?"

She nodded tearfully.

"All right, then we need to get Jim back to the hotel. I'll call you tomorrow."

"I can send the limo around…" The man said, but Evan shook his head.

"Our SUV is parked right outside. We can get him through the crowds and out of here quicker."

"Give me your keys, I'll have Barney let me drive a little closer," Matt said. Evan tossed him the set from his pocket. "Mr. Aames—remember what I said about when you leave here."

Bennet nodded. "Yes, thank you, Mr. Haight."

The other man, Shane Lowry, returned with coats and purses and bags, lugging them like a caddy. "Come on, the limo is out back, and the paps are being held in the front. We need to leave now."

Daisy threw her arms around Griffin, who hugged her back with one arm—the other securely around Jim's middle. Evan caught the bulk of his weight, his arm draped around the other man's back. He fought back the feelings of being uncomfortable and kept his professional face on.

"I'll call you tomorrow, promise," Griffin said, kissing the woman on the top of the head. She was then bustled off between the two men and out the door, her feet barely touching the floor.

"I'm never going to a play again," Jim mumbled.

Evan drove them to their hotel; Matt got out and spoke to the manager about a back entrance to get them up to their room. Jim didn't want to walk through the lobby looking beat-up—which Evan totally understood.

Evan also understood Jim could deal with this. It was near routine in his mind, a reflex action that resulted in some bumps and bruises. No big deal.

Griffin, however, hadn't said two words since the theater, and now, even as Matt and Evan helped Jim onto the bed, he was silent.

"I'll get you guys some ice. The manager is sending up coffee and water and some extra towels," Matt said.

Jim mumbled something and toed off his shoes, sinking into the pile of pillows behind him. Evan glanced at Griffin and saw the trembling taking over his slender form.

"Hey, Griffin, let's go into the other room for a second—Jim, you just call if you need anything," Evan said.

Griffin followed, running his hands through his hair as he walked the length of the suite.

"Uh—you need anything?" Evan asked, watching as the young man tugged at his hair.

"Why are you being so nice all of a sudden?"

Evan blinked.

"I'm concerned about you and Jim. That must've been pretty scary."

"Scary? No shit. All of a sudden I see this crazy guy jumping at Daisy, and Jim's right there, stopping him and throwing him down, and the guy—the guy just goes nuts, screaming and punching, and then it's over, and I…" Griffin stopped, gasping for air. "I realized he had a gun. Jim got a gun away from him."

Evan nodded slowly. "You've never seen anything like that before, I'm sure."

"Understatement." Griffin's knees got wobbly, and he sat down on the couch, hard. "So right now I'm running on a continuous loop of what would have happened if Jim hadn't gotten to him in time and he killed Daisy, or what if he had gotten Jim while they were struggling, and then I kinda want to throw up." He put his head in his hands and shook.

Evan sat down on the coffee table in front of him, close enough to be comforting but hopefully not intrusive.

"Neither of those things happened."

"They could have."

"Yeah, they could have, but they didn't. And that moment is over, and you can move on. Worst-case scenarios about the past aren't really going to help you. Or Jim."

Griffin sighed. "Yeah."

"And I'm—I'm sorry it took this for me to be nice to you." Evan cleared his throat.

"Yeah. This is sort of one of those perspective things, right?"

"Right." Evan smiled in spite of himself. The door behind them rattled and opened, with Matt and the filled ice bucket being followed by a rolling cart. Evan turned around and noticed Matt frowning.

"What's wrong?"

"The security in this place is shit," he said, putting the ice bucket down on the table. "I don't want reporters trying to get up here."

"There are reporters at this hotel?"

"Yeah, and they probably followed your friends too."

"Shit."

Evan stood up and tipped the waitstaff who were listening and watching as he shooed them out the door. "You might want to change hotels in the morning. How long are you here for?"

"We're booked here until Wednesday, then we were going to make a decision on going home." Griffin looked back toward the bedroom. "I'm going to check on Jim. If we're changing hotels, it won't be until Jim feels better."

Matt nodded. "Yeah. I hate leaving you guys without a line of defense, though."

Evan saw the vulnerable expression on Griffin's face and the look of concern on Matt's and made a decision—the only one that made sense at the moment.

"Matt, why don't you stay here tonight—sleep on the couch. That way Griffin doesn't have to worry about anything but Jim."

He got a double look of surprise.

"Tomorrow we'll figure out where you should go. Maybe we can find a private residence for you instead of a hotel, so there won't be records."

Matt was smiling at him—still calculating in his head but smiling. Evan smiled back.

"Great idea. If it's okay with you, Griffin."

"Sure, thanks." Griffin got up and started walking back toward the bedroom. "I'm going to check on Jim and probably just stay in there so—thanks for staying Matt, and take whatever you need and, uh, Evan—thanks. A lot." He gave them a wave and closed the bedroom door behind him.

"He's freaked out. Make sure he gets some sleep," Evan said—then felt Matt's arms go around him.

"You may be a jealous dick, but you always come through in a crisis," he murmured, and Evan returned the embrace tightly.

"I'm sorry about dinner. The stick in my ass was poking my brain, and I didn't remember my manners."

"Lovely visual, thanks." Matt kissed him on the mouth. "I'm still kinda pissed off, but I don't have the energy to deal with it now."

Evan nodded. He deserved it. "Fair enough. Let me note again—really, really sorry. No excuses."

"True." Matt sighed. "Will deal with it later. I have to keep my head in this game for the moment."

Evan gave Matt a sincere smile. "You want me to stay?"

"Nah, I got this. And I don't think you're gonna want to leave the kids all alone the whole night."

Evan shook his head—he hadn't even thought of that. "Well, there goes Dad of the Year again."

"Shut up—I'll call you in the morning." Matt kissed him again, and when he would have pulled away, Evan deepened the kiss, angling his mouth to delve his tongue deeply around Matt's.

They separated slowly, and Matt's eyes fluttered open with a question in them.

"Thanks for putting up with me," Evan murmured.

Matt shrugged. "I love you. What else am I supposed to do?"

"I'm trying—just know that."

"Me too."

"What are you trying to do?"

"Curb my need to throw you down on the couch and do dirty things to you?"

Evan blushed and took a step back. "You're on guard duty."

"When I'm off duty?"

"I'll see you at home."

Evan slept alone in his bed that night, for the first time, he realized, since he and Matt bought the house.

He hated it.

He rolled over, face down, trying to shut out the cavernous emptiness of the room without Matt. He tried to sleep, but the tension of the evening, the sudden shift in emotions—meeting the infamous Jim—it kept him awake.

The infamous Jim of the phone calls and the one-night and the book. Ridiculously good-looking and smooth, and so very much in love with young Griffin Drake. When Evan had gotten over the fact that his "competition" in Matt's male lover category was gorgeous, he'd had to contend with his own uncomfortable envy of the way Jim and Griffin interacted in the restaurant.

They were a couple—no apologies, no glancing around to see who was looking, no hiding their relationship. And here was Evan, nearly jumping out of his skin whenever Matt came too close.

He tried to imagine taking Sherri to dinner and treating her like a business acquaintance. He tried to imagine living long enough to try and explain to her he didn't want complete strangers knowing about them being in love.

Shame coursed through him.

Evan thought he'd taken such a huge step when he invited Matt back into their lives. But he was realizing that he hadn't gone all the way.

He needed to be entirely honest with himself before he could expect to be honest with Matt. Or his kids. Or the rest of the world, for that matter.

Evan tossed and turned until daylight crept into the bedroom. Still so many questions and not enough answers.

Chapter Thirteen

The squad room hit its usual Monday morning madness level by eight a.m. Burning on only a few hours sleep, Evan was on his second cup of coffee, running names through a database, when a shadow loomed over his desk.

"Evan Cerelli?" a man's voice asked.

Evan looked up at the young uniformed officer and nodded. "Yes?"

"Hi, I'm Jesse Masters with GOAL."

Evan extended his hand. "GOAL?"

"Gay Officers Action League. We're a fraternal order of criminal justice professionals. I wanted to introduce myself."

He glanced around to see if anyone was watching or listening; his fellow detective Moses was the closest to his desk, and he was very clearly listening.

"Nice to meet you." Evan stood up and glanced around, wondering if there was a private space they could took.

"Chris Callas gave me your name—I hope you don't mind."

"No, no, of course not." Evan tried to remember if he knew Chris was a lesbian and realized he had no clue one way or another. Helena never mentioned it.

"I was hoping you might be able to make our next monthly meeting. Second Tuesday of every month at The Center on West 13th Street."

"Meeting? Gosh, I don't know, to be honest. I have a commute to Queens and four kids to get home to." Evan smiled politely. "But if you have a card or something I'll definitely keep it in mind."

Jesse reached into his uniform for his wallet and pulled out a card. "Yes, please. I hope you'll consider it. We have a great group of people, lots of events and gatherings. There are many families, so we'd love it if your kids and your partner could join us."

For a split second Evan thought "Helena" but realized that Jesse meant Matt.

And for a moment he was afraid.

But Jesse was still smiling, young and friendly, so clearly hoping that Evan would agree to come to his group's meeting. Evan looked down at the card in his hand. "Second Tuesday, you said?"

"Yes, that's right. If you need directions or have any questions, please feel free to give me a call."

Evan extended his hand. "Sure, Jesse—thank you. I'll let you know."

As he watched the young man turn and leave, Evan felt eyes strong and steady on his back. He turned and gave Moses a glare.

"Can I help you?"

Moses shrugged. "Nah. I was just eavesdropping. Heard everything I wanted to."

Evan resisted the urge to give him the finger.

"How's Jim feeling?" Evan asked when he called Matt a few hours later.

"Sore and grouchy. I'm pretty sure the latter is a fairly constant thing. Griffin said it's a sure sign he's okay."

"How are you doing?"

"I want my toothbrush and clean underwear." Matt sighed through the line. "But Griffin's still jumpy, and I'll feel better when they're checked into someplace no one knows about."

"About that—Helena's mom's place is a studio, but she's been staying at Vic's, so it's free."

"Tsk, tsk, kids today. Living in sin. Doing it like fiends before they even exchange vows…"

"Boss. Best friend's mother. Please refrain."

"Puritan."

"Is that a yes on the studio? I can drop off the keys during lunch."

"Personally drop off the keys? I'm going to say yes just to be able to see you."

"I saw you a few hours ago!" Evan protested, even as he smiled.

"I hate sleeping without you, okay? I miss your snoring."

"You're very romantic." Evan caught Moses' eye and bodily turned, lowering his voice. "I'll be there by one thirty. With the keys."

"Will you stay long enough for me to cop a feel?"

"One thirty. And I'll also bring you a toothbrush."

"Now see? That's romantic."

Evan murmured an "I love you" and hung up, swinging his chair around to face Moses.

"Am I really that interesting?"

"Nah, not really." Moses went back to the files on his desk, leaving Evan frustrated, something immediately noticed by Helena as she returned from a meeting.

"What's the bee in your bonnet?"

He gestured toward Moses, who waved in response.

"Whatever. Did you talk to Matt?"

"Yeah, they're going to take the studio. You have the keys?"

"Uh-huh. You dropping them off?"

"Yes."

"I'm going with." Helena sat down and turned her computer on.

"Why?" Evan's suspicions were raised.

"Because I want to meet Jim."

"Oh hell no."

"My mom's apartment, my keys to give, I want to go and meet him."

"Why in God's name?"

"Dying of curiosity. I want to see the guy that makes you spit with jealousy every time you hear his name."

Evan slammed a drawer open and closed for effect. "I'm past that."

"Ha!"

"It's true." Evan lowered his voice. "I'm trying to have some perspective on this whole thing, and I think I've achieved it."

"Ahahahaha." She slapped the top of her desk, drawing a few turned heads. "Oh my God, you are lying to yourself."

"Okay, personal discussions in the workplace over. Illegal gambling operation files opened and being discussed."

"You act like this is over. I still have the keys." She pulled them out of her purse and jingled them like she was coaxing a baby to smile. "You will tell me all about this perspective on the way over."

When Evan arrived at the hotel suite—with a smirking Helena in tow, he was flustered and irritated, a state that only increased when the door opened courtesy of Shane Lowry and revealed a veritable crowd of people.

Bennet Aames, Daisy Baylor, Jim, Griffin, and Matt were all sprawled on the various couches with the remains of lunch spread out on tables behind them. Bennet and Matt in particular were deep in conversation.

"Come in—Good to see you again, Detective," Shane said as he ushered them in. He shot a glittery smile at Helena. "Shane Lowry."

"Detective Helena Abbott," Helena said smoothly, her voice kicking down a notch.

"Pleasure." Shane shut the door behind them. "Can I get you folks anything?"

"No, thanks." Evan finally caught Matt's eye, and his boyfriend rose to greet him.

Shane went over to pour himself some coffee, and Helena leaned close to Evan.

"Quite the swanky group," Helena whispered. "That's Shane Lowry, the playwright."

"Why do you know that?" Evan whispered back.

"He's always in the gossip section. Playboy type." She fluffed her hair.

"Hey, hi." Matt leaned in for a quick kiss, stopping midway. Evan completed the movement for him, registering the surprise in his face.

"Hey, we brought the keys." He pointed to Helena. "She made me bring her."

"Want to meet everyone?" Matt smiled as Helena nodded eagerly.

Matt brought them over, and another round of introductions were passed around. Evan noticed Jim looked a bit better this morning, even as the bruises were more pronounced. Griffin had an exhausted air about him, and Evan felt himself grow concerned. All this noise couldn't be good for either of them.

"So I have a little time if you want me to help you guys move over to the studio," Evan said to Jim.

"Sounds good." The older man didn't look at all pleased with the sprawl of people in the room. "We already packed our stuff."

"We have the sedan," Helena reminded Evan. "It's not going to fit everyone."

"Oh, I'll give Mr. Haight a ride over. He and I have some business to discuss." Bennet Aames seemed to say everything like a grand pronouncement. He smiled at Evan. "Your boyfriend has some excellent ideas regarding security."

Evan received a spate of glances from everyone except Shane and Daisy, who were oblivious to Evan's general discomfort with public commentary on his romantic status. It didn't bother him—not really—and he smiled.

"I'm sure he does. We'll go on ahead and meet you there, Matt."

And then it was just packing up and moving out. Jim moved slowly with Griffin and Evan back on point and Helena leading the way, with a bellhop and the cart of luggage and Matt bringing up the rear. They moved swiftly down the back service elevator and to where Evan's car was waiting.

"Hey, we got this down pat," Matt said as he helped Jim into the car. "Anyone want to join the Secret Service with me?"

Evan remembered something and walked around to the car to present Matt with a toothbrush, freshly wrapped in plastic and a tiny tube of toothpaste. "See, I remembered," he said with a smile.

"Awww, thanks." Matt gave him an affectionate shot in the arm.

"See you at the studio in a bit?"

"Yeah. I don't think Bennet will take too long with his pitch."

"Pitch?"

"Last night I gave him some suggestions, stuff I picked up when I worked for the security company. He seemed into what I was saying. So today he shows up and starts asking me if I would consider doing bodyguard work."

"Seriously?" Evan stuck his hands in his pants' pockets. "Like—bodyguard to the stars?"

Matt shrugged. "I guess so. Jim saving the day last night made him think he wants someone around Daisy all the time. Jim's not based out here or he'd ask him, and since I used to be a cop…" Matt's voice trailed off. "I didn't say yes or anything. I'm just going to listen."

"Of course." Evan thought Matt would be a great bodyguard from a professional perspective. From a personal standpoint, the very thought threatened to curl his smile into a frown. "Yeah, you should definitely listen."

Matt looked at his watch. "You better get going. I'll see you at the studio later. Or home—whatever."

"Okay. Yeah. See you later."

Matt didn't even try to kiss him good-bye on the busy sidewalk, offering instead just a little wave and then heading back toward the service entrance.

Evan watched him go, conflicted in a hundred different ways.

Evan and Helena got Jim and Griffin settled in the neat fourth-floor studio. There was plenty of food to keep them inside without need for deliveries or going out. Everything was fresh and tidy and far more private than a hotel.

They waited for Matt, even tried his cell a few times, but Evan eventually had to admit that his boyfriend was still mired in business with Bennet.

"So call if you need anything," Evan told Griffin. "And please go get some rest. Jim's on the mend; you need to sleep."

"Right." Griffin leaned on the door frame, sagging under the weight. "I'm going to go do that. And thanks a lot, Evan."

"You're welcome." He glanced at his watch. "I have to get back to work. When Matt stops by, tell him I'll see him at home."

"Sure." Griffin smiled wanly. "I, uh—I'm sorry I was a snot to you at the restaurant. Jim told me that you were kinda uncomfortable about being out and like—not out? So I'm sorry I was poking you."

Evan flushed, embarrassed. "It's okay. I deserved it. I'm sorry if I made you uncomfortable."

"The making out at the table—totally unplanned, I swear."

That made Evan smile. "Actually it made me a little envious."

Griffin looked surprised. "Well—Jim was supposed to tell Matt to tell you this before he played action hero, but if you ever need to talk or something about…you know, stuff, I'm a really good listener. And talker, but you probably already knew that."

"I did." Evan paused a beat. "And thanks. I might just take you up on that. But not until you sleep."

Griffin saluted. "Deal."

"Chris Callas is a lesbian," Evan heard himself saying as he drove he and Helena back to the station.

"Uh, right. I kinda already knew that," Helena said.

"Why didn't you tell me?"

"Was it a vital piece of information missing from your life?"

"No, but you could have said something."

"Why?"

"What do you mean why? I'm—I just thought you might mention it."

Helena "whatevered" him under her breath. "So how did you find out?"

"She gave my name to some gay organization for criminal justice employees."

"She did?" Helena's eyes got wide.

"Which then begs the question—how did she know about me?"

"Is that a leading question because you already know the answer?"

"You told Chris Callas I was…" Evan paused, glancing over at Helena.

"Gayishly bisexual because you had a wife and now you have a boyfriend." Helena lifted her chin defiantly.

"Gayishly bisexual?" Evan rubbed his forehead with the palm of his hand.

"What? You can't even discuss it without stuttering, and we all know how you hate labels," she said—complete with hand-gestured theatrics. "I needed to come up with something."

"They want me to join the group."

"Then join! Chris said they're nice people, and they do good work. It's a nice support network."

Evan sighed as he pulled into a parking space in front of the precinct. "Being…out…at work is something I didn't really consider, Helena. You knowing, Vic knowing…"

"Moses knows. So does Kalee. And Nicole in Records—her dad is friends with Lenny." Helena started ticking people off on her fingers. "And if Nicole knows that means Gina in the lab knows, and quite frankly if Gina knows, people in Alaska know you live with a man."

Evan banged his head on the steering wheel.

"What? Who cares? They knew you were married." Helena got out of the car, completely cutting off Evan's "it's different" argument.

He kept it to himself, because he knew what her response would be.

"Why is it different?"

Evan followed her into the building, glancing here and there at fellow cops and office workers on the sidewalk and in the entranceway.

Did they know he lived with a man?

Did they care?

Chapter Fourteen

Matt managed to leave a quick message for Evan about being home late, then did the same with a call to the house phone and a text to Katie's cell. Everyone had keys, walking wouldn't kill any of the kids—it would be fine.

He stopped fussing and followed Bennet through the shopping mall he called an apartment.

The thing was huge, the entire floor of a pre-war on the Upper West Side. Their footsteps actually echoed on the hardwood floors. Matt tried to remembered to keep his jaw from dropping open.

There was also the matter of the limo that drove them here—and the doorman, the housekeeper, the "staff" who helped Daisy get settled into her suite and offered Matt an assortment of food and beverage while he waited in the foyer for Bennet to make sure Daisy was resting comfortably.

This guy probably took baths in money like Scrooge McDuck.

"She's drifting off. The sedative helped," Bennet said as he entered the room. The dark suit jacket and tie were gone, giving Bennet what Matt guessed was his "casual rich dude look."

"Good to hear. She's, uh—she's had a stressful few days, huh?"

Bennet sighed. "Yes, she has. Shall we go into the parlor?" He led Matt one room over into an ornately gold and black-schemed sitting room. "Daisy has lived a bit of a sheltered life. I have to fight myself not to fall into that same overprotective trap."

Matt glanced around the magazine-layout mansion and cleared his throat. "Right, gotta keep it real."

The other man snickered as he sat down across from Matt on one of the sofas. "It's okay to think I'm ridiculous. Sometimes I think I am as well." He crossed his legs. "Believe it or not I grew up in a Philly housing project with my mother and brother."

Matt whistled. "You're pretty young to have gone from that to this."

"I was extremely fortunate. My mother had very strong opinions on education and focus. She made sure my brother and I lived up to that expectation."

"What does he do?"

"He's a heart surgeon." Bennet grinned. "Which makes me the very rich, very successful runner-up in my mother's eyes."

"I'd say it sucks to be you but…"

"It doesn't." Bennet winked. "And now that you know a bit about me, I'd like to make you an offer."

"Don't you want to know about me?" Matt rested his elbows on his knees. "I mean, you just met me…"

"I had my assistant run a background check on you this morning."

"Wow, you don't mess around."

"No, I don't. I'm very careful about whom I allow in my inner sanctum. It's part of the reason for my success, quite frankly." He brushed his hand across his trousers. "I like the way you assessed the situation the other night. I like the way you offered suggestions based on your concern for Daisy's safety. That impressed me."

Matt shrugged. "Once a cop, always a cop."

"Which is why Daisy is unharmed right now—because Jim was there, and his reflexes, his eye for the out of place. A former cop would be ideal for this job. Not to mention a background in security as well. You're perfect."

"I've never been a bodyguard, and I—I don't know if I'm looking for a full-time gig." Matt resisted the urge to check his watch or cell phone.

"You have other responsibilities?"

"You're the one who ran the background check," Matt said flatly. "You have to know I live with Evan Cerelli, and he has four kids."

"So you're the main caretaker. That's very interesting," Bennet said conversationally. "Have you adopted them?"

"Huh? No." It hadn't even occurred to Matt why he would do that. "They have a father."

"True. But he's a police officer. If something happened to him in the line of duty…" Bennet put up his hand. "Please excuse me. I shouldn't have said that. It was unthinking of me. Honestly I have this on my mind because of a situation a friend went through."

"What sort of situation?" Matt thought about Evan being injured a few months after they met. How his in-laws had swooped in and taken the kids; he had no say, the kids had no say.

"He and his partner were raising a child, biologically his partner's… Well, his partner was killed in an accident, and in the middle of all the grieving, his partner's parents announced they were taking the child back to Florida." Bennet's voice cracked. "It was awful. There was nothing he could do. They have the rights; he did not." He sighed. "Again, I'm sorry. I shouldn't have said anything. I'm tired, and it's been on my mind."

Matt felt numb. His hands tingled, his ears buzzed.

"No, I'm glad you said something, actually—it's important to think about," Matt said, trying to regain his equilibrium.

"To get us back on track—I'm willing to offer you one hundred fifty thousand dollars a year plus expenses and insurance to come work for me. You'll be solely responsible for Daisy's well-being."

Matt blinked. "That's a lot of money."

"I have a lot of money. I spend it on what matters most."

"I have to think about this. It's going to involve late hours, traveling. That might not be workable."

Bennet nodded, sitting forward. "Of course. I don't expect an answer right away. In the meantime, I'd like you to assist me on a retainer basis. When you have time."

"Sure." He gave into temptation and checked his watch. School was just getting out. "I really need to go home and shower, change my clothes. I'll give you a call tonight."

"Good enough." Bennet stood and offered his hand. "We'll talk later. Let me call the driver so he can take you back to Queens."

It started raining halfway through Matt's limo ride home. He knew the twins didn't have umbrellas and hit the auto dial for Katie's cell phone.

"Hi, where are you?" Katie huffed without even saying hello.

"Stuck in traffic. Where are you?"

"Waiting for the twins. It's pouring. God, my hair is a mess."

Matt cursed under his breath. "Stay at the school. As soon as I get to the house I'll pick up my car and drive over there."

"Too long to wait. We'll walk. It'll be fine."

"Katie, please just wait for me. I'll be there as soon as I can."

She agreed begrudgingly, and they hung up. Matt leaned forward and tapped on the glass.

"Hey, listen, you think Mr. Aames would mind if we made a detour?"

Any guilt about being made to wait in the rain was erased when he picked up the kids in the limo.

They delighted in pressing buttons and stealing soda from the fridge. Katie caressed the lush leather seats and squeaked.

"I need to talk to the career counselor at school," she said.

"Why?"

"Because I need to know what major I have to have to make this kind of bank."

"This kind of bank?" Matt stopped Elizabeth from standing up and hitting her head. "No more urban music for you."

"So you're friends with a rich guy now? Can we have a pony?" Katie took a Pellegrino from the fridge.

"He asked me to work for him; this is my ride home from the interview." Matt shifted in his seat. He wasn't expecting to have this conversation with the kids before a) thinking it over and b) talking to Evan. Their wide-eyed stares made him nervous.

"You're getting a job?" Elizabeth asked. She looked decidedly unhappy.

"Hey, people work while their kids are at school, you know. It's not like we're babies," Katie said helpfully. "I'm sure it wouldn't be too much of a difference."

"What about summer time? Or after school?" Elizabeth looked at Matt. "What about if we get sick?"

"I'm not going to some stupid after-school program," Danny announced, and that was all he had to say on the matter.

"Hey, slow down. He made an offer, and I'm supposed to think about it." Matt didn't mention the traveling or late hours. "No one is going to any after-school program just yet."

Elizabeth seemed mollified, but Katie's appraising look made him glance away out the tinted window.

People with kids worked all the time. If he wanted to they could figure it out—and it would be something that was just his. Separate.

"Mom didn't work," Katie said as she sat down next to Matt at the kitchen table. He was trying to drink a cup of coffee and read the paper, but she brought a can of diet soda and clearly wasn't leaving until they talked.

"I'm not your mom," Matt pointed out.

Katie traced a pattern on the table. "You sorta are."

"No, actually I'm not." Matt pushed the paper away and reined in his tone. "I'm not legally anything."

"Who's talking about legal? I'm talking about you being the person who's here for us."

"Well maybe I need to do something else and remind everyone I'm not the mom."

Katie frowned. "That's stupid. I thought you enjoyed it."

"I like taking care of you kids—I do." Matt rubbed his eyes. He hadn't slept enough to have this talk with Katie. "I'm just thinking about getting a job, that's all."

The frown deepened. "Are you and Daddy breaking up?"

"No, of course not! Nothing's wrong." Matt laid his hands over hers. "I'm not going anywhere."

“Right, okay.” Katie's hands were cold under his. “Okay. Well—good luck with deciding about the job.” She pulled her hands out from under his and got up, leaving her soda behind as she drifted upstairs.

Matt sighed. The television was blaring as Danny played his Xbox. Elizabeth he could see on the deck, kicking around in the puddles left by the sudden rainstorm.

He had dinner to get ready and things to consider. Like whether there was enough money in the world to lever him out of this house.

A nap sounded like a great idea, until he heard a key in the front door lock, and Miranda Cerelli—the eldest and most dramatic of all of Evan's children—flew through the door with a fierce look on her face.

“My grandmother is going to try and get custody of the kids,” she seethed, slamming the door behind her.

Chapter Fifteen

Evan knew something was wrong three steps into the front door. It was ridiculously quiet at half past seven, and Miranda was sitting on the sofa, an angry expression on her face.

“Oh God, what?” he asked as he dumped his briefcase.

His eldest folded her arms over her chest. “Grandma came to see me at the dorm.”

An inward groan subdued, Evan took his suit jacket. “What happened?”

“She said that her and Grandpa wanted the younger kids to live with them, and I quote, 'Get them out of this house of sin.'” She air quoted. “And she wanted to know if I would testify.” Miranda tsk-tsked. “She wanted me to talk to her priest.”

“Now she's got her church involved. Wonderful.” Evan muttered to himself as he sat down catty-corner to Miranda. “Can I ask what you said in response?”

Miranda smirked. “I feel vaguely powerful right now.”

“This is kind of a serious matter, so I'm not joking,” Evan said quietly. “I need to know what you said.”

His daughter looked surprised and then a tad offended. "Like I would testify against you? Whatever I think about you and Matt is an opinion, but I wouldn't put the younger kids through something so ugly."

"Whatever you think about Matt and I?" Evan's fingers wound tightly together. "Can you elaborate?"

"Sure—it's weird and confusing since you were married to Mom for like—ever. You have no idea what sort of stuff people say behind your back and what they say to Katie and Danny and Elizabeth at school. It's not easy, okay?" Miranda's arms tightened, and she gave herself a hug. "But I still don't think Grandma and Grandpa should be raising the kids."

"Thank you." Evan cleared his throat. "And I'm sorry this hasn't been easy for you."

"It's fine. Whatever." She jiggled her legs nervously. "It's weird coming home and it not being home. No, Mom, no same old house."

"I know. Sometimes I miss it too," he said, honest and raw as his throat began to hurt.

"You have Matt now, and the kids have someone to take care of them, but I—I don't have Mom. I can't call her to talk about stuff that's going on like…like boys and school and the future. Who am I going to go to when I get engaged or married? Who's going to plan my wedding with me and…" Miranda's voice cracked. "I miss Mom and I hate Grandma for putting me in the middle."

Evan got up and sat down next to Miranda, sliding his arms around her. He caught the first tear against his shoulder and rubbed her back in gentle circles. The process of comforting her kept his own tears at bay.

They sat in silence after her crying jag ended. He realized somewhere in the middle of the quiet that no one else was home.

"Where're Matt and kids?" he asked finally.

Miranda blew her nose on a tissue. "Matt took them to dinner. When I got here I was all pissed, and I told Matt what Grandma said." She bit her lip. "He was kinda upset."

"I'm sure," Evan murmured. He patted her shoulder and got up to get his phone. "He didn't call."

"I think he just wanted to get the kids out the door."

"Right." Evan scrolled down and hit Matt's name on his contact list. It rang a few minutes, then went right to voice mail. Evan redialed.

"Maybe he shut his phone off?" Miranda said helpfully.

Voice mail again. Evan hung up and glanced back at his daughter. "You know I need to call your grandmother about this."

Miranda sighed. "I know. She's going to be pissed at me for telling."

"She has no right to be. She also has no right to come to your school and bother you about this."

"I think she means well, Dad. Seriously. She just misses Mom so much, like we do. But she can't move on."

Evan scrolled up and hit Ellie's number. He needed allies before making the next call.

"I know, and I'm sorry for that. But this isn't about her or me or your mom. This about what's best for my children."

Ellie was exasperated as Evan explained the day's events to her. He could hear her relaying the story to Walt through the phone.

"There's a new priest at her parish. He seems to be a bit more radical than Father Deckard. Maybe he's pushing her for this custody thing."

"Ellie, seriously—I'm not going to let it get to that point." Evan's nails dug into his palm as he paced the living room. "Katie and the twins are not going through the spectacle of a court case because your parents can't accept facts."

"Evan, I know. I'm on your side," Ellie said. "I don't want it to get to that either. I'm just saying—she's... It's all she's got right now. My dad is barely sober these days," she added, sadly. "The hope that she might get the kids is what's keeping her going."

"That is not my problem." Evan glanced around to the kitchen, where Miranda was making tea and listening to the conversation. "The kids are well taken care of, loved, and healthy. The only problems are in her head. I don't want to do this, but I will end contact between her and the children if it comes down to her not abiding by my wishes."

Ellie went quiet. "That would be cruel. The kids are all she has left of my sister. They're her only grandchildren."

"I don't want to be a jerk here, Ellie, but the threat of a custody battle is unacceptable." His teeth gritted. Everything in his body hurt from the strain of keeping his temper in check. “Asking Miranda to testify against me? Un-fucking-acceptable.”

A car pulled into the driveway; Evan looked out the window and saw the twins and Katie getting out of the minivan, with Matt not far behind.

“I know.”

“The kids and Matt are home. I'll talk to you in the morning.” Evan hung up on Ellie, knowing he'd be apologetic the next time they talked, but for right now, all he could see was bright red fury.

“Daddy!” Elizabeth's voice was followed by a solid *thunk* against this middle. His youngest hugged him tightly, burrowing against him. He hugged her back, just as tight.

“Hey, sweetheart, how was dinner?”

“We went to the diner. And mini-golf,” she said, looking up at her father with those wide doe eyes. “Is Miranda still here?”

“In the kitchen, squirt,” her eldest sister called. Elizabeth disengaged and ran to her sister with the same physical greeting.

Danny slunk in and gave his father a strange look. “Hey.”

“Hey. You all right?”

Danny shrugged. “Not doing day care, not going to court. I mean it.”

Evan nodded, perplexed by the day care but reassuring his son nonetheless. “Agreed. It's fine. Your grandmother's just doing what she thinks is best.”

Katie and Matt finally reached the door, heated whispers breaking off as they saw Evan. Danny took the pause as a cue to disappear into the sunroom.

"His grandmother..." Matt muttered, but Evan held up his hand. Matt shut up.

"This is crazy," Katie said. She was clearly trying to keep it together, but the adult/child war going on for the sixteen-year-old was starting to list to the latter's side. Her eyes filled with angry tears. "Totally crazy. She can't really do anything right? They can't take us away?"

"No, they can't take you away." Evan put his arms around Katie; she rested her head on his shoulder. "You're sixteen. You can decide who you want to live with."

"So they would be fighting for custody of Elizabeth and Danny?"

"No, they're not fighting for anyone or... Just don't worry about it, okay? Your grandparents do not have the right or the legal precedent or the money to make this a reality. It's just a threat."

Matt said something under his breath and stalked off to the kitchen. Evan tried to catch his eye, but it was impossible—and Katie needed him more at this moment.

"They need to stop, okay? I don't want to talk to them ever again if they don't stop." Katie cried against his shoulder, and Evan's stomach turned, anger boiling up again. It would be a fitting punishment for him to keep the children away from Josie and Phil entirely.

"Hey, calm down. It's okay. I'll talk to her in the morning, and we'll get this straightened out," Evan murmured, stroking her hair. "Calm down." He could feel the tremors running through her body—this wasn't normal Katie behavior. "Hey, did your grandmother contact you as well?"

"No." Katie wiped her nose on her sleeve. "She makes little digs on the phone sometimes, but I ignore her."

"Then why so upset? You know better—she can't take you away from me."

"Yeah, she could. If you got hurt or something, like last time? If you were in the hospital—we had to go with her. She's our legal guardian if something happens to you."

"Is that true?" Miranda said from the kitchen. She had Elizabeth on her lap, her small frame barely able to fit the growing nine-year-old against her shoulder and not topple over. "Grandma and Grandpa are still our legal guardians?"

"Yeah," Evan said slowly. Matt's jaw twitch was visible enough to be seen across two rooms, and Evan caught a bit more of the clue bus. "I didn't change my will after your mom—after your mom passed away. They're still legal guardians."

It was set up that way when the kids were babies, the "just in case" clause because of Evan's job description and Sherri's parents' insistence. He was young at the time, with no family of his own. Of course, they were the obvious choice. But times had changed, and he no longer considered the pair appropriate.

Frankly, if something happened to him, there was only one person he truly could imagine taking care of the little ones.

And that person was standing on the other side of the first floor, steam all but coming out of his ears.

"I'm going to have to change that—as soon as possible," Evan heard himself say. "I'll call the lawyer first thing, and we'll take care of it," he repeated, kissing Katie on the top of the head. "Your grandparents won't be your legal guardians."

"Then who will be?" Miranda asked. There was a level of challenge in her voice.

Evan cleared his throat. "Matt. And your Aunt Ellie. If something happens to me, they'll take care of you."

Elizabeth unburrowed herself from Miranda's shoulder. "But we'll live here, right? With Matt?"

"Right, of course." Evan didn't hesitate. And this time the look he shared with Matt wasn't an angry challenge. It was the receipt of a look of surprise.

Elizabeth was mollified by the answer, as was Katie. She gave him a final squeeze, then muttered something about needing a tissue. She went upstairs after exchanging looks with Matt.

"Come on, Elizabeth. Let's go upstairs and wash your face," Miranda said, shooing her little sister off her lap. She gave her father a pointed glare.

"You're too young, and you know it, so don't even start, okay?" Evan read the look perfectly. "Talk to me in ten years."

"Fine." Miranda herded her sister upstairs.

Evan's knees gave out, and he sat down hard on the easy chair.

"Fuck me," he wheezed, hands covering his face.

He heard Matt approach, felt the cold bottle touch his wrist. He peered out to see a slightly shell-shocked Matt standing there with a bottle of beer.

"So hey, how was your day?"

"I haven't slept in like two days—legally I'm a danger to society." Matt slumped down onto the nearest couch. "I used the worst profanity in front of your children today when Miranda showed up and told me what happened."

"Forgiven." Evan drank a hearty sip of the beer, then put the cold glass to his forehead. "I'm really going to enjoy calling Josie tomorrow to politely threaten her with never seeing the kids again."

"That's sarcasm, right?"

Evan sighed. "Yeah, sorta. Because I can't do it. I just can't. She's out of her fucking mind with grief, and chances are it's going to be that way until she dies. If I take the kids away from her… I'm not that cruel."

"I am." Matt kicked the coffee table. "Fuck 'em. All they do is guilt-trip the kids and make them uncomfortable."

"They're family."

"What does that even mean? Put up with shit you wouldn't take from a stranger because of DNA? Such bullshit."

Evan smiled sadly. "Yeah, it is. But I still can't do it, Matt. I'm going to lay down some law for her, and we'll hope it sticks. When the kids get older, they can make a decision about whether or not they want contact."

Matt huffed and puffed, punched a pillow for good measure.

“Stop that. I'm giving you legal guardianship of my kids—I need to know you can control your temper.”

Matt's eyes narrowed. “You're serious?”

“Of course. Why? Don't you want to be their legal guardian?”

“No, I want the chance to dump them at the first opportunity and run to Aruba with your life insurance money.” Matt poised himself on the edge of the couch. “It's a big step.”

“You see them more than I do. That's a big step. Paperwork is just…”

“A legal and binding document that says I'm your choice to raise your kids.”

“Right. Because you're the person I trust most in this world. And the person I love. And the one who I know will protect my kids as fiercely as I would.” The words came from a deep well in Evan's heart as his voice softened. “It makes sense.”

“Okay.” Matt looked at the rug, the ceiling, the picture over the fireplace. “Okay.”

“Okay.” Evan finished his beer. “I need to go check on Danny. Maybe eat some dinner.”

“Leftovers in the microwave, coming right up.” Matt still wasn't looking at him.

Something gnawed at Evan. “Why did Danny mention day care? Do you know?”

“I picked the kids up in Bennet Aames's limo since I was late. They asked so I said I had a job offer.” Matt cleared his throat.

"That was quick." Evan's stomach did a flip as he finished his beer.

"Quick and sexy. He wants to give me a ton of money to play bodyguard to Daisy Baylor. Serious bank, as Katie said." He rubbed his hands together and stood up. "The kids weren't thrilled."

"They love having you around."

Matt frowned. "They miss their mom. They need someone here, and I'm their only choice."

"Or you know—they love you." Evan stood up, and Matt moved again, heading for the kitchen. "Where is this coming from?"

"A long day and no sleep." Matt rummaged around in the refrigerator. "Plus Liz is the most irritating headshrinker in the world. She puts too many thoughts in my head."

"Huh? What are you thinking about?" Evan put his hand against Matt's back, drew him around.

"It's a long story." Matt pushed a foil-covered bowl at Evan and evaded his attempt at an embrace.

"So tell me the story." Evan shut the door and put the bowl on the counter. He didn't let go of Matt's arm, because suddenly he realized they both needed grounding.

Matt's dark eyes burned, and Evan could see the weariness. "You don't want to be gay, but you want to be with me. You don't want other people to think you're gay, but you'll give me your kids—your kids, the most important thing in the world to you, because I'm the guy you love. Sometimes I wonder—sometimes I think this is just an exercise in stupidity, you and me. You wouldn't be worried about labels or custody battles or anything else if I wasn't here." Matt stopped and shook his head. "I am so fucking confused at the moment, you have no idea. Because I don't want to leave, Evan, but sometimes, sometimes I think it would just be fucking easier if I did."

"Don't say that." Evan's hands clenched against Matt's shirt as his heart tightened painfully in his chest, and he pushed himself closer. "You need to be here."

"No, I don't *need* to be." Evan could feel Matt holding himself back.

"You're worth it, okay? Whatever we have to figure out..." Evan took a breath and paused. "Whatever I have to figure out—it's worth it. I can't do this without you. Hell, I don't want to do this without you."

Matt relaxed, a tiny increment of release, and Evan closed the distance between them to nothing.

"Maybe it matters a little bit—what I label myself," he whispered, his mouth hovering near Matt's. "Maybe it matters what other people think, and I need to live with that. I can't make everyone happy."

"No, you can't. And why the fuck would you want to?" Matt said, resting his forehead against Evan's.

"I want to make you happy," Evan smiled. He let the kiss bloom out of a gentle touch, opening his mouth for Matt as their bodies fit together comfortably.

"You're gonna call the lawyer tomorrow," Matt murmured as they drew apart.

"Yeah. What are you going to tell Mr. Aames?"

"I think I have to tell him thanks but no thanks. Unless he plans to give me the limo for all school pick-ups."

Evan soothed each of the kids individually, taking a few bites of dinner between conversations. Matt disappeared onto the back deck for a while with his cell phone; when he came back in he appeared a bit more relaxed.

"Mr. Aames?"

"No. Jim. He's feeling better—and he wants to get the hell out of Dodge, but Griffin has some meeting tomorrow, so he's stuck here for a bit."

Evan put the empty bowl in the dishwasher. "How's Griffin?"

"He sounded okay. Said to remind you to give him a call." Matt sat at the counter and gave Evan a raised eyebrow look. "Do I want to know?"

"We, uh—made amends that night when Jim got hurt. He told me to call him if I needed to talk." Evan wiped the counter down; he could feel a flush heating his skin. "I was thinking of taking him up on it."

"Do I even want to know what you'd be talking about?"

"Just—things. In general." Evan threw the dish rag in the sink. "Things I can't really discuss with anyone else."

"Such as…" Matt made a rolling motion with his hand.

"Such as—I don't know. Listen, I don't have any gay friends, and maybe I'd like some perspective on things."

Matt looked shocked enough to tip over with a feather. "You're seeking a gay perspective on something?"

"Yes." Evan reached into his pants and pulled out his wallet, fished around for Jesse's GOAL card, and threw it on the counter. "Gay Officers in Law Enforcement. I think there's a picnic in a few weeks. Maybe we'll go."

Matt pretended to fall off the stool.

"You just used the word gay like six times without flinching."

"There was inside flinching. A little," Evan admitted. "But I think I'm doing okay."

"I'm shocked."

"Don't be." Evan picked the card up and put it on the fridge by the calendar of all importance. "Just—enjoy the baby steps."

Chapter Sixteen

Griffin was standing outside Serena Abbott's apartment building when Evan pulled the sedan up after work two days later. He honked, and the younger man waved, sliding his BlackBerry in his pocket as he reached for the door handle.

"Sorry I was late. Meeting ran over," Evan said by way of a greeting as Griffin put his seatbelt on.

"No problem. I was just talking to Bennet on the phone." He didn't look pale or stressed anymore; that cheeky enthusiasm Evan caught the first night at dinner had returned. "So you probably don't care because you're a cop person and not a showbiz person, but he's really into my script, and I think he might make me an offer." Griffin bounced a little in his seat.

"That's good, right?" Evan pulled into traffic as Griffin sighed dramatically.

"I need to get back to Hollywood where someone cares."

"An offer is good—I'm guessing that means money?"

"It means I can make this movie the way I want to and not sell my soul to a big studio." Griffin adjusted his sunglasses against his nose. "And yeah, a shitload of money."

"Mr. Aames seems to be on the loaded side."

Griffin whistled. “You have no idea.” He tapped his fingers against his khakis. “Jim said he offered Matt a job. Taking care of Daisy.” He was clearly curious.

Evan pulled up at the red light and nodded. “Yeah, but I think it might be a little more commitment than Matt's interested in.”

“Daisy is a full-time job,” Griffin said drily.

“Mr. Aames seems to have volunteered for the job.”

“Yeah. I don't quite understand that deal at all.”

“What?”

“Do you really want to hear this? It's like—crazy gossipy relationship crap.”

“I have teenage daughters, I can handle it.” Evan pulled into a parking garage and slowed as they cruised down the ramp.

“I think I'm insulted,” Griffin muttered as they got out of the car.

In the small dark Irish pub Evan had selected for this early dinner, the lunch crowd was gone, and the supper crowd wasn't anywhere to be seen. Even happy hour didn't seem to be carrying much steam. They sat a small corner booth.

“So are you going to tell me?” Evan asked as he looked at his menu. He wasn't sure he cared, but it was easier to listen than to force himself to actually utter the questions he had lurking in his skull.

“You asked for it.” Griffin put his elbows on the table. “I've known Daisy since we were kids, and she has literally the most hideous taste in men ever. Her ex-husband was a massive tool, all her in-between extracurricular boyfriends have been residents of Loserville, and her most healthy relationship to date has been with me."

"You and she?" Evan's eyebrows went up.

"Not like that—like…married without sex or passion or anything physical." Griffin sighed. "And even that got pretty screwed up. So when she picks a guy, you just have to know there's something wrong with him."

"There's something wrong with Mr. Aames? I thought you were hoping to work with him?"

"Work with him, not date him." Griffin gratefully accepted water from a bus boy and took a giant gulp. "Daisy, meanwhile, is apparently not only dating him but living with him."

"And there's something wrong with him?" Evan asked again.

"Well yeah, there's the small problem that he's gay, and she's talking about marriage!" Griffin sat back in his chair, incredulous. "Seriously—she's telling me they're getting married and talking about kids…yada yada yada… Meanwhile he's gay."

"Maybe he's…" Evan struggled for a moment. Changed his mind? Experienced something new and surprising. "Maybe he's not entirely gay."

"Not entirely gay?" Griffin made a face, then bit the inside of his mouth. "Oh right, sorry."

"I believe the proper term is bisexual," Evan said quietly.

"Yes. Yes, it is. But—" Griffin bit off his words. "It just sounds far-fetched. He's got this major player rep on the East

Coast, and all of a sudden, boom! He meets Daisy Mae and that's it."

Evan put down his menu. "It happens. You think one thing the majority of your life and then that changes."

"I really don't want to be fifty and suddenly want to sleep with women." Griffin drank the rest of his water. "No offense."

"None taken."

The waitress finally realized they were sitting in the corner and popped over to offer drinks and take their order. Evan demurred on something from the bar, but Griffin ordered a double martini.

"I'll behave, I promise," he said as she walked away.

"Good, glad to hear it." Evan played with the napkin for a moment. "And I hope for your friend's sake that she and Bennet are truly happy together."

"Hmmm, yeah. I try not to worry about her, but I can't help it. It's second nature," Griffin said sadly. "She's an awesome person for all her faults. I just don't want to be her keeper anymore. I have Jim, and I like concentrating on taking care of him."

"You don't seem to be his—keeper."

"Nah, it's not the same thing. It's actually much nicer to go home to someone who isn't sometimes a life-draining emotional vampire." Griffin cleared his throat. "I say that with love."

"Of course," Evan smiled. "Jim's a—he seems like a very nice guy."

"And you hate his guts."

Evan held up his hand. “I never said…”

“You didn't have to. That night at dinner I thought you were going throw down at some point. Just…boom—right in the mouth.” Griffin made a fist.

“I would never punch him,” Evan said, uncomfortable now.

“Probably not, but you did think about it. Come on, it's okay. You're jealous.” Griffin's voice dropped conspiratorially. “Me too.”

“Of Matt?”

“Hell yeah. You know, Jim doesn't talk to any of his exes. Not a one. I couldn't even get a damn name out of the man. But Matt's his pal. That's kinda…”

“Weird.”

“Yeah, weird.” Griffin smiled. “But okay. I'm really okay with it. It's stupid to imagine being with only one person in your whole life.”

Evan huffed a smile of his own. “Not that stupid. For some people, it's a goal.”

“I guess. So you—you were with your wife for a long time?”

“Almost twenty years from when we first met.”

“And you never dated anyone else?”

“No, not until Matt.”

Griffin whistled. “Wow.”

“But weird.”

"Twenty years with a woman and then a guy? That's pretty intense." Griffin looked at him speculatively. "Must've freaked you out."

"In ways you can't even imagine." Evan sighed. The conversation was segueing where he needed it to go even as he fought the urge to move it away.

"Oh I can imagine!" Griffin chuckled. "I always knew I was gay—or I should say, I never had a question, just the answer. Like I imagine most straight people just know they're straight. It was okay, till I started learning about sex. I mean—straight sex, shocking enough, but the rest of it? I was like—no way, seriously." Griffin cracked himself up. "I briefly considered celibacy."

"Then what happened?" Evan took a deep breath.

"High school boyfriend, slightly older with apparent access to a lot of information." Griffin smirked. "He liked to play master/apprentice, and I got a good education."

"So you and he…" Evan gestured, then blushed. "You did…everything."

"Everything ever? No. I was willing, but I also had a lot of homework junior year."

Evan rolled his eyes. "You know what I mean?"

"Yeah, I do, but it's kinda fun to tease you." Griffin smiled sweetly. "You cop types, Jesus Christ on a pony. You're all so damn uptight. And you're in vice, for heaven's sake! You must've busted a few rings of like…stolen sex toys or something."

"No. No, I haven't." Evan's cheeks burned.

"You should. That would make an excellent porno. Speaking of which…" Griffin's voice dropped way low even though there was no one in sight. "You know, if you're like—looking for information or stuff, a good porno cannot be counted out. You have to remember these guys are professionals, and the first few times it's not that awesomely fun, and also most guys aren't hung like that. But you know, it's good information."

Sweat pooled behind Evan's ears. Oh this was a mistake. "I already have—seen. Several things."

"Good, good. I mean, I'll admit it. The first time I was like—no freakin' way. Just blow me or something." Griffin caught himself and coughed. "But patience can be a good thing."

Evan resisted the urge to crawl under the table. His curiosity still burned. "So you got used to it?"

"It?" Griffin shrugged. "Yeah. But that makes it sound like a chore." He waggled his eyebrows. "And it's not. Especially when I figured out what I wanted."

"So you've done…both." Evan shrugged out of his suit jacket, letting the cool air of the fan hit the back of his neck.

"Sure. Best way to figure out what you like. And I like to mix it up now and then, but with Jim…" Griffin paused. "Okay, if I say stuff that's personal, you're not going to freak, right?"

"No, I'm not going to freak. Just—go easy on the descriptive words."

"Okay, sensitive soul—with Jim, it just fits. What he needs and wants and what I need and want—they fit. He doesn't care if I never want to, uh, okay, does 'bottom' work for you as a descriptor?"

Evan died a little but nodded. "Sure."

"Good. So—he doesn't care if I never want to because what works with us is me on the top and him on the bottom and various other stuff." Griffin's smile was teasing. "You want like little sketches on my napkin?"

"No."

"Did our waitress go to Iceland for my vodka?" he asked, looking over Evan's shoulder.

"So Jim likes… Jim is…" Evan's voice cracked.

"Yeah." Griffin crumbled up his napkin and threw it at Evan's head. "Come on now, no stereotyping please. He's older and bigger and hot like burning fire and I'm a nerd in glasses, so that's not possible?"

"I never said that!"

"But you kinda thought it."

Evan picked the crumpled napkin from the floor. "It is a stereotype, and sometimes when you don't have a frame of reference…"

"Fine, whatever. You're excused, but don't make the same mistake again." Griffin shook his head. "I mean, what if I met you when you were married to your wife and assumed you were a giant abusive asshole—because cops have a rep sometimes? What would she have done if I said that?"

"Given you an earful." Evan smiled and ducked his head.

"As well she should. Maybe I'm right and maybe I'm wrong, but I should probably wait until I have more information than just shit I've heard from people who don't know. And oh, thank God. This better be the greatest martini ever."

The waitress didn't apologize for the endless delay, leaving their drinks and a bread basket before disappearing again.

"Eat up, this may be the only thing we're getting." Evan sighed.

"I'll make do." He slurped down half his martini with a happy sigh. "Brilliant. Too bad I'll never see her again to ask for another." He gestured toward Evan with his glass. "How am I doing with the help thing?"

"Pretty good," Evan admitted. "It's kinda nice to talk to someone about this stuff."

"What's next?"

"I think I'm okay for now. Thank you."

Griffin pouted. "Aw, come on. Ask me something really dirty so I can watch your forehead turn that color of burgundy again."

* * *

Evan dropped Griffin off on the same corner and waited until the younger man entered the building. He rested his forehead on the steering wheel with a sigh.

Oh that was an informative dinner. And he was sure he'd burned out a few brain cells from the sheer heat of his blushing. From the bottom of that empty martini glass came the sexual wisdom of Griffin Drake, very few holds barred. He had suggestions and tips, and "did you put a pillow under your hips? It'll help," almost caused Evan to develop heart palpitations.

Which of course Griffin absolutely loved.

His phone buzzed, and he checked the number to make sure it wasn't Griffin with something he'd forgotten to share.

No, it was Ellie, and he pressed the call button with a frown.

"Ellie? Everything okay?"

"Yeah, everything's fine. I just wanted to let you know my mother and I had a… Let's call it a talk for the moment." Ellie sighed deeply.

"Was it bad?"

"Epic and ugly."

Evan turned off the car and leaned back, checking his rearview mirror for the meter readers.

"And?"

"And she got the papers about you changing guardianship. Then she called a lawyer."

Evan's heart dropped into his stomach. He gasped.

"Who told her she didn't have a case," Ellie continued, her voice tired and gentle. "Then I spoke to Father Deckard, who went to the house, and—it was just a mess. She's hysterical."

Evan regained his voice. "I'm sorry, Ellie. I really am."

"I told her to stay away from the kids for a while and then we'd do something in a few weeks, her and I with them for a few hours. I told her I didn't want her alone with them."

"That must've gone over like a lead balloon."

"She's just stuck in her grief and anger, Evan. I can't get her out." Ellie's voice broke. "Father Deckard and I are trying to get her into counseling."

"I hope you can, for everyone's sake."

"Right." Her tone wasn't hopeful. "Walt said I can't move this mountain and that we have our own life to live, but you know, I'm all she has now."

The burden was heavy, clearly.

"You still have to have some boundaries."

"I know."

"Remember, Walt is there for you. And I am—as best I can. I mean, the kids are my first priority, but we're still family."

Ellie sniffled. "Thanks, Evan. I just wanted to let you know what was going on."

"Thanks, Ellie."

They hung up, and Evan's chest squeezed out another stuttered heartbeat.

* * *

That night in bed, Evan stared up at the ceiling as Matt feigned sleep beside him. Finally at two a.m., Evan rolled over and poked his boyfriend in the side.

"What? I'm sleeping," Matt grumbled.

"Me either."

Matt sighed and turned his head. "What's wrong?"

"Nothing. Or you know, everything." Evan kicked his legs under the blankets. "I will fucking head for the Canadian border if my in-laws try to take my kids," he said.

"I'll drive," Matt said simply.

"Okay." That made him feel a tiny bit better. He reached under the covers, hands moving restlessly over Matt's chest. "You wanna…?"

"Want to what?" Matt asked drily, already wiggling out of his shirt.

"Shut up," Evan muttered. He lifted the covers off Matt's body, suddenly ravenous for some physical contact. His mouth sank down over the flat brown nipples, hair tickling his nose as he teased the tiny bud one side to the other until Matt shifted.

"Zero to a hundred." Matt moaned and rolled over toward Evan, scissoring their legs together.

Evan didn't say anything, he just moved lower, hands pulling at the waistband of Matt's boxers.

He didn't let Matt slow it down, didn't let him undress Evan as well. He got Matt naked and under his hands, under his mouth as fast as he could, the bed shaking below him at the effort.

"Turn around," Matt moaned. "Let me suck you."

But Evan shook his head. He swallowed Matt down frantically, tight fingers on his hips.

At the last second, he pulled off, leaving Matt straining against him, begging for just a little bit more.

"No," Evan whispered. He swung one shaky leg over Matt, positioning himself over him. For one confused moment his boyfriend froze under him, and Evan almost lost his nerve, but then he leaned down for a kiss and settled over Matt.

It took a moment of coordination, but then Matt's hard, wet dick was pressed against his stomach and Evan rubbed the length of it against his ass. And that's when Matt's startled moan told him his idea was fucking brilliant.

Matt's hands closed on his hips, keeping the pace. Evan held onto the headboard and rocked, the tease of flesh from root to tip rubbing him intimately as his own dick brushed wetly against Matt's chest.

"Touch yourself," Matt whispered, and Evan didn't hesitate for a second. In the dark bedroom the bed creaked, and Evan jerked himself off as his boyfriend rutted up against him in a frantic attempt to come. It didn't take either of them long. Evan shook in a desperate attempt to hold on as Matt stiffened and a warm, wet sensation covered Evan's ass. But it was too much.

He couldn't wait. He stroked down hard and leaned back, feeling Matt's hand cradling his lower back as he shot against his lover's chest.

Evan slept after that. Four solid hours with Matt draped over his back, pinning him to the mattress. It felt so good he cursed the alarm when it started beeping.

"Pencil me in for Saturday night," he murmured to his boyfriend as he got out of bed.

Matt mumbled something in his sleep.

Evan took a ridiculously cold shower and tried not to stare at the predatory expression in his eyes in the mirror as he shaved.

He dialed Jesse from GOAL's number after nine and got directions to the meeting. The young officer was clearly delighted at his acceptance. Evan wrote it down in his datebook and set an alarm on his phone.

He was going to go.

When Moses got up for a coffee refill, Evan followed him and shadowed him for a moment as they filled their cups.

"Everything okay?" Moses asked, his dark face curious as always.

"Yeah." Evan dumped some sugar into his cup. "I wanted to know if you had anything to, uh—say or… I know you've heard about my living situation."

Moses's eyes widened, and he snorted, clapping Evan on the back. "Evan, my God, you've been living with Matt for what? Almost a year? Are you just getting around to giving out announcements?"

"No, this isn't an announcement. I just wanted to make sure it wasn't an issue." Evan put his shoulders back and looked Moses in the eye.

The older man shrugged. "None of my business. Just like knowin' what's going on."

"You don't have an opinion?"

"Why would you care about my opinion?" Moses looked genuinely surprised. "Like I said, none of my business. Just do your job and watch my back when you have to."

Evan wanted to poke him until he said something—approval, disapproval. Sometimes. But Moses refused to offer anything else. Evan couldn't even read his expression.

"That's it?"

"That's it." Moses shrugged, took his coffee, and returned to his desk.

Evan felt strangely relieved by their exchange.

He stopped by Serena Abbott's apartment during his lunch hour. Griffin buzzed him up.

"Hey, glad you stopped by." Griffin opened the door, and Evan stepped inside the small studio. Jim was in the kitchenette pouring coffee.

"I wanted to say good-bye before you left. Matt said you're flying out in the morning." Evan and Jim exchanged nods.

"Yeah, I have some revisions to do now that the screenplay is optioned," Griffin said delightedly.

"Act excited," Jim called, and Evan smiled.

"Glad to hear it. Congratulations."

Griffin gave Jim the finger over his shoulder. "Thank you, thank you. We're going to fly back to Seattle, maybe drive up to stay in Tacoma for a bit. Jim's going to start fishing."

"I didn't say yes yet."

"It's either that or crocheting as your post-retirement hobby. Pick one."

Jim grumbled as he walked into the living room. The bruises had mostly faded, and his hand was no longer bandaged. "Your fine city has been a real pain in the ass, and I can't wait to go back to the left coast."

"Sorry about that." Evan put his hands in pockets. "I hope next time you two visit it'll be a bit more relaxing."

"We'll have to redo the dinner thing," Griffin said. "I think we all deserve a do-over on that one."

"Agreed." Evan felt Jim eyeing him and cleared his throat. "Griffin, would you mind if Jim and I had a moment alone to talk."

"It's a studio—where do you want me to go?"

Jim motioned toward the bathroom. "There must be more time you can spend on your hair."

"Ugh, fine." Griffin bear hugged Evan before he could politely refuse. "Give me a call anytime. I have more dirty doodles for you."

And with that, Griffin exited the room.

Jim looked after him fondly.

"You have quite the boyfriend," Evan said. "He was really kind to have lunch with me and, uh—I appreciate it."

"That was all him," Jim said, a bit sternly. "He couldn't stand you feeling bad."

"I know. And I can't stand letting you go back to Seattle thinking I'm a complete prick," Evan smiled. "I'm sorry for my behavior that first night. I brought every one of my issues to the table, and that wasn't fair."

"You know Matt loves you, right? That I'm no threat in any way, shape, or form?" Jim sighed. "And maybe it's not for me to say but even when he and I were together that one time—you were there too. He was just—missing you. And I happened to be there, that was all." Jim gave him a serious glare. "Please tell me you get that. I don't want to stop talking to Matt over this, but I will if it's going to cause problems again."

Evan shook his head. "It's not. I'm done with that." His mouth curled into a smile. "Though I'll be honest, this would all be easier if you were uglier."

"Well it would be easier to dismiss you as an asshole if my boyfriend didn't insist you were just tragically misunderstood." Jim finally cracked a smile.

Evan stuck out his hand, and Jim clasped it. They shook, firm and solid.

"Thank you," Evan said, sincerely. "I'm grateful you took care of Matt when he needed it."

Jim looked momentarily embarrassed. "He did the same for me."

"Good." Evan meant it. He let go of Jim's hand and nodded. "Well, I have to get back to work. I hope you'll come back to New York for a less dramatic stay."

"Probably around the holidays!" Griffin yelled from the bathroom.

"Probably around the holidays." Jim sighed. Evan coughed into his hand to hide his laughter.

"Let Matt know and we'll set up a dinner. You can come out to Queens, meet the family."

"Deal."

Jim showed him to the door, and they gave each other a parting, knowing smile.

"Take care of him," Jim murmured.

Evan nodded and went on his way.

Chapter Seventeen

Matt came down from his post-workout shower Saturday afternoon and found the house perfectly, eerily quiet. No television, no half a cell phone conversation, no Xbox or stereo. Just the ticking of the wall clock and the hum of the ceiling fans.

"Hey, is this like an episode of the *Twilight Zone*?" he called, checking around the first floor.

"Which one?" Evan came in from the deck.

"Well clearly not the one where everyone disappears. Where'd the kids go?"

"Ellie and Walt picked them up for the weekend. They'll be back tomorrow night." Evan was casual but deliberate in the kitchen, putting a pitcher of iced tea and two glasses on a tray.

"When did these plans happen?" Matt smoothed his T-shirt nervously.

"I called Ellie yesterday afternoon."

"Did I forget something we had to do?"

Evan smiled and flushed, charming the absolutely shit out of Matt.

“I thought we could take advantage of the empty house,” Evan murmured. “Spend the day in bed.”

Matt leaned against the counter. “The whole day.”

“Well we don't have to.” Evan matched Matt's posture. “But if you wanted to…”

“Is this the return of horny beach house, Evan?” Matt drawled, hoping the answer was yes and hoping beyond all hope that the outcome would be very different.

“Nah, it's an improved version.” Evan straightened up and came around the counter, his walk slow and languid. Matt swallowed a moan.

Matt reached for him, but Evan kept just out of his grasp. “Come on. Upstairs. If we start downstairs we'll get distracted.”

“I don't consider sucking your dick a distraction.”

Now it was Evan's turn to smother a groan. “I do. I'd rather have your mouth somewhere else.”

The words were sexy; the blush on his lover's face just made it that hotter. Matt took a step toward the stairs. “Hurry up before I can't walk.”

He kept his hands to himself until they were in the bedroom.

Evan was already undressing, his breathing shallow and eager. Matt thought he might be having the greatest sex dream of all time—but the chill of the air in the curtained room as he pulled off his shirt told him it was all very real.

There were things on the nightstand, noticeable as Evan flicked on the lamp. He pulled down the cover, got an extra pillow—Matt blew out a breath as Evan crawled onto the bed.

He gawked, and Evan smiled up at him.

"You're being a little too calm about this," Evan murmured. "I'm starting to get nervous. Excuse me—more nervous."

"I'm trying not to jump you," Matt said, kneeling on the edge of the bed. "I don't want to mess this up."

"We do pretty well with everything else. It's just adding something, right?" Evan sprawled on the bed, opening his legs and spreading his arms in invitation.

Matt's IQ dropped a hundred points. His mouth went dry as he trailed a hand up Evan's leg, tracing a loopy circle on his inner thigh.

"Right. Just something extra."

Evan's legs opened wider.

"What did you do?" he whispered, unable to take his eyes off this intimate posture.

"Research." A sheen of sweat popped across Evan's body.

"Oh yeah? And what did you decide you wanted?" Matt crawled over Evan, pushing his legs wider with his knees.

Evan reached up and traced Matt's mouth. Matt chased his fingers with sharp, needy teeth, but Evan didn't let him catch a taste until he was ready.

"Go slow," was all Evan said, so low and quiet that Matt saw the words more than heard them. He sucked two of Evan's fingers into his mouth, eyes closing as he simulated his best blowjob.

Evan's body vibrated beneath him, inside him. He let the spit-slick fingers slide out of his mouth, feeling the trail of cool wetness as Evan traced a line down his chest, his hand curved around Matt's cock.

"Just a little," Matt exhaled, already rocking into Evan's hand. "I'm gonna need that."

Evan didn't disagree; he stroked, slow and steady, wet fingertips playing over the head. Matt murmured encouragement before he started to pull away—just enough to keep himself in check.

"My turn." Matt glanced at the night table to see the lubricant and condoms. He reached for the tube, apprehension flitting through his head until Evan moved restlessly under him.

"Don't take forever," he whispered, and Matt didn't waste any more time.

His hands shook, with excitement and nerves. The sticky wet lubricant spilled out on his fingers.

"Use a lot, and take your time and…" Evan's breath was shallow. He licked his lips.

"Shah," Matt said. He kissed the center of Evan's chest, mouthing a damp circle on his warm flesh as his hand slid under his ass. Evan froze, but Matt kept going, moving in tiny increments until he touched the vulnerable pucker of skin.

Evan shivered. His hands went to Matt's shoulders, not pushing or fighting him off but holding on for dear life.

Matt rubbed his fingers in easy circles and pushed the tiniest bit, the gentlest of pressure. He kissed down Evan's stomach, opening his mouth to take the head of his dick against his tongue. His fingers pressed deeper, and Matt swallowed convulsively to keep himself in check.

He kept this up, the easy sucking, the pressure and circling of his fingers. He listened for hesitation or a stop from Evan, but there was nothing but encouraging moans and bitten-off curses.

Matt lifted his head and shifted lower on the bed.

Evan lifted his legs and opened himself to Matt intimately.

It was a second too much, and Matt reached down to hold himself in check before this was over too soon.

He said nothing as his mouth joined his fingers in their teasing preparation.

He held his dick the entire time, as he tasted Evan's body and drew the pleasure out until they were both rocking the bed in anticipation.

"Roll over," Matt finally murmured, biting and kissing the inside of Evan's thigh.

"Pillow," Evan choked as he disentangled himself from Matt.

"Under your hips," Matt finished as he stroked Evan's back. It was slow, and Matt eyed the condom package with wariness; he was terrified the touch of the damp latex would send him shooting before he ever got inside Evan.

"Yeah." Evan shook as he lay down, moaning as his rock-hard dick touched the pillow.

"Like this," Matt whispered, opening Evan's legs again. The position was erotic, his lover absolutely beautiful sprawled out on their bed. "I'm going slow," he said. He rubbed his hands over Evan's strongly muscled back. "Just tell me if you need to stop."

Evan nodded, his fingers curling onto thc covers.

Matt bit the inside of his cheek as he opened the condom's case and slicked it onto his dick, counting and breathing to get it down to the root without losing it.

He kissed the small of Evan's back.

He opened him and kissed the intimate hidden part of him.

He pushed his tongue in and pressed in and found a rhythm that Evan responded to in a second.

He pulled back when Evan cried out.

He held his cock, breathed through the pounding excitement in every fiber of his being and pressed the head where his tongue and fingers had opened.

"Breathe, relax," Matt choked. The tightness drew him in even as he paused in worry. "Relax."

Evan shook beneath him. He gasped as if in pain, but he pushed back, and Matt instinctively pushed forward.

They both paused.

Matt pushed again.

Evan moaned loudly, restless against Matt as he pulled closer to the bed, then back again. Matt let him move, let him have this second of control as he held himself still.

Another inch. Another push. Matt's fingers were white against Evan's hips as he felt the internal pressure of his lover's body open to him.

Another inch. Matt looked down to where their bodies were joined and rocked his hips in a frantic motion.

Evan wailed.

Matt stopped as much as he could even as he pushed in a little bit more, and like he'd zapped his boyfriend with electricity, Evan writhed around him and the stream of sound began.

"OhGodohdon'tjust… Right there," Evan begged, shaking and sweaty beneath him.

"Like that?" Matt's voice was hoarse.

He rocked.

Evan cried out, and one hand frantically slid beneath him.

"Oh yeah, that's right. Touch yourself, baby," Matt crooned as he rocked, not entirely inside but enough for both of them. The pressure of Evan's tight body clamped down on him, the erotic sight of them being joined, the frenzied motion of Evan's hand as he jerked himself off. Matt held on and rocked and shifted until the bed smacked against the wall and pictures rattled on the nightstand.

"Uhhhh." Evan's body seemed to erupt, and Matt rode the inner pull of his body through the orgasm, the scent filling the room. He managed a few more shallow thrusts before his balls drew up, and he pulsed into the condom, into Evan.

He grabbed the headboard to keep from falling over, grabbing the base of the condom before pulling out. Evan moaned weakly, and Matt rested his forehead against his lover's shoulder as the condom came off into his hand.

"Fuck are you okay? Oh my God." Matt exhaled. He thought he might have broken something vital and important in his chest as he struggled to get enough oxygen into his lungs.

Evan just moaned again.

"Tell me you're okay, so I can fall over," Matt whispered, and Evan nodded, turning his head slightly.

"Holy shit," he whispered, and Matt took that as an invitation to pitch onto his side.

Evan eventually rolled over, his face flushed red and his mouth struggling to find a way to form words. He lay against Matt's shoulder, aftershocks lingering on his skin. Matt could feel them.

He licked his lips, waited for a reaction.

"Can I ask if it was good for you?" he croaked.

Evan shook his head and laughed weakly. "I—I don't even know what to say. I couldn't stand up right now if I needed to."

"It was, uh—intense." Matt licked his dry lips.

"Felt…strange at first, and then"—Evan looked away—"then it felt so good I think I lost my mind."

Matt's chest puffed up.

Evan elbowed him in the side.

"Listen, I don't want to freak you out or anything, but I might want to do that like—all the fucking time." Matt sighed. The room smelled like sex. He felt like a god.

He got another elbow.

They did leave the bedroom a few times. A shower, dinner downstairs. They walked around in their boxers, and Matt was worried he was going to have a permanent erection as Evan loaded the dishwasher in his underwear.

"You're crazy," Evan commented as he set the controls.

"What?"

"You're watching me like I'm doing something sexy. When what I'm actually doing is housework."

"I'm sorry I find you stupidly hot." Matt rubbed his chin. "Do me a favor?"

"What?"

"Just stand there and show me your arm—so I can see your tat..."

Evan rolled his eyes. "Like this?" He turned his arm so Matt could see the inside of it, traced the USMC lines with two fingers.

Matt shifted in his shorts.

"Can I ask you to do something else?"

"I think I already told you bare-assed in the kitchen was not my thing," Evan said. He shut off the light over the sink and walked past Matt to the staircase.

"Can we do bare-assed in the bedroom again?"

Evan paused. "You know, I—I enjoyed it, okay? But I'm a little sore."

Matt almost swooned. "You should have said something—I'll kiss it and make it feel better."

This time Evan was the one who had to shift in his shorts.

* * *

Sunday night came and found them sleeping on the couch—clothes on, for the first time since yesterday. Matt was tucked against the back of the couch, Evan lying next to him. It was warm and cozy, and thank God Matt couldn't get it up one more time—he was fucking exhausted.

"Should we talk about anything before the kids come home?" Evan asked drowsily.

"We need milk?"

"Not what I meant."

"Fortunately for you I'm middle-aged and I can't get it up all the time, so you will have some breaks,"

"Closer." Evan opened his eyes, those baby blues that got Matt into so much trouble in the first place. "I needed this to happen on my terms."

"And it did—right?" Matt shifted slightly, his hand on Evan's chest.

"Yeah, it did." Evan smiled. "I was just explaining—I'm glad I didn't force the issue before."

Matt nodded. "It wasn't a deal breaker; it never was. This doesn't complete our relationship or elevate things. It's just fucking awesome."

Evan snorted. "God, you're a walking erection."

"For your ass's sake, be glad that isn't true. You'd have to quit work."

“Have I created a monster?”

Matt mock growled.

They heard the doors of a car open and shut outside, the noise of the kids coming up the walkway and to the front door.

“Quiet naked time over.” Matt sighed as Evan disentangled and sat up.

“Hiiiii, we're home,” Elizabeth slammed into the house and ran over to jump into Evan's lap. “We had a great time. Did you miss us?”

“Were you gone?” Matt threw a throw pillow playfully at her head.

Ellie and Walt brought in the rear as Katie and Danny were bickering over something; there were questions about food and did anyone want coffee. Evan stood up and went into the kitchen.

Matt lay on the couch with a dopey smile on his face. He just couldn't help himself.

Chapter Eighteen

Bennet poured Matt a drink at the bar and handed him the heavy cut glass filled with amber liquid. It wasn't like Matt was expecting Bennet to crack open some brewskis, but still—he sniffed before he took a sip.

"So I'm curious what you decided, Matt." Bennet didn't waste time getting to the point. He sat in an elegant chair, legs crossed and black eyes narrowed in the other man's direction. "Will you take the job with me?"

"This is going to sound crazy, because frankly you're offering me a shitload of money, but—I'm needed at home." Matt sank into the creamy white cushions of the sofa. "The kids aren't ready to be alone, you know?"

"No, actually I don't." Bennet said with a laugh. "But one day I hope to. I suppose I can appreciate your devotion to family. If you won't do the everyday detail, I was wondering if I could impose on you some consulting work. We could work our meetings into a schedule that wouldn't conflict with your other obligations."

There was no irony or derision in the man's tone and that sealed the deal for Matt.

"Consulting, I can do. I'm guessing you mean security and not…" Matt gestured at the opulent space Bennet referred to as his "office."

"Decorating."

"I don't know, I'm thinking of going suburban man cave next season," Bennet said drily. "But yes, security consulting. I'm building a new place out on the island, and I'd like it to be as safe and secure as humanly possible."

"You don't mind me saying, I think you're going a tad overboard with the security thing. I know what happened to Daisy was scary, but…"

"I know I seem overcautious, but Daisy means the world to me, and second only to that is my privacy. I've long since existed mostly under the radar, but now—well, now the spotlight seems to be shining in my direction."

"Good for your career."

"Bad for peace of mind." Bennet sipped his drink. "Will you help me, Matt? I promise to make it worth your while."

"Done. And don't worry—we'll find someone to watch Daisy twenty-four seven if need be. She'll be fine."

They finished up a bit more business, and though Matt tried his best to demur, Bennet pushed a check into his hand for their "meeting." Matt resisted the urge to choke when he saw the tightly scripted numbers written out on the pale blue paper.

He dialed Evan's cell phone as he waited for the valet guy to bring his car around.

"Hey, wanna have dinner tonight?" he asked before Evan could get out anything but a hello.

"We have dinner every night," Evan said, and Matt eye-rolled the wall of the garage.

"I mean, you and me, out alone for dinner."

"The kids…"

"Can order Chinese and watch television without our presence. Come on—it's Friday night. Date night."

"I…" Evan seemed to hesitate, then sighed. Matt held his breath just a little bit. He knew things weren't entirely settled, but they had to start somewhere. Dinner on a Friday night—sans children and with a big check—would be a good place to start.

"Okay," Evan said finally. "I should be home around seven."

"Perfect."

* * *

Matt gave the kids fifty bucks and made them sign blood oaths to behave like little angels and not call unless someone was unconscious. Their eyes wide at the wad of tens, they all three nodded and swore.

"I think I'm almost ready to buy a car," Katie announced as she pocketed her share.

"I still want a pony," Elizabeth said.

Danny mumbled something about his own place.

He took a shower and changed into a respectable outfit, a date outfit frankly, dark jeans that fit well, and a long-sleeved button down with a leather jacket.

He even used aftershave.

Katie whistled when he came downstairs, and Matt tried not to blush.

"Dad just pulled up," Elizabeth announced from the deep recesses of the easy chair.

Matt checked his reflection in the toaster.

"Hey," Evan called from the front door. He greeted the kids and fielded questions and comments before making it to the kitchen where Matt was waiting awkwardly.

"Hey," he repeated, blinking as he looked over Matt's outfit. "You got a date tonight or something?"

The smile was small but there, and Matt returned it. "Yeah, he's kind of the jealous type too, so if you don't mind going upstairs before he arrives…"

Evan had the good grace to blush.

"Give me fifteen minutes and we'll be out the door."

"Deal."

Evan started to turn, but he crossed the kitchen to lay a kiss on Matt's mouth, lingering and promising at once.

Half hour later they were cruising down the boulevard, their hands resting against each other on the console.

"You didn't say where we were going." Evan finally broke the silence.

"Dinner."

"But where?"

Matt rolled to a stop at a red light. "You sound like one of the kids," he said affectionately, stroking his fingers over Evan's wrist.

Evan humphed at that, but he leaned closer to Matt, his body language speaking to a yearning that made Matt want to forget about dinner entirely.

"It's nice, I promise."

Actually Matt had been thinking a fancy place on the Upper West Side, but he made a change of plans in his head as they pulled into traffic. It was probably the most romantic idea he'd had in a damn long time.

The traffic into the city was light, and the music on the radio filled the companionable silence. Evan seemed relaxed—but clearly curious as he tried to gauge where they were going.

"Hey, this is…"

"Yeah."

Evan and Matt parked on the street; there was a familiar site on the corner.

O'Malley's.

"First date memories," Matt teased as he opened the door. The stale smell of peanuts and beer hit him, an old familiar friend. Evan shook his head but stepped inside.

"God, how much money did we spend here?" Evan murmured as they walked automatically to the back to see if their table was free. It was.

"Bad beer and wings are not cheap, my friend." Matt took off his jacket and sat down. "And I have a pocket full of cash. We're gold tonight—go ahead and order mozzarella sticks."

"Big spender."

Matt rested his elbows on the table and looked around. It seemed a hundred years ago he and Evan would come here a few times a week to commiserate over their lives, literally crying in their beer over the sad state of affairs.

Tonight it was a lark, a memory revisited before they went home together.

Crazy.

“Never thought those two guys would end up being us,” Evan said, smiling through the dim light.

“Quite a shocker,” Matt agreed. He felt Evan's leg press against his under the table.

“Not sorry.”

“Me either.”

Matt's hand snuck under the table, brushing over Evan's knee.

“I might miss that apartment you had—with the mattress on the floor,” Evan said shyly, leaning into the touch.

“Very sexy,” Matt nodded. His fingers played with the seam of Evan's trousers.

“We didn't have any idea what we were doing.”

“I'm still not entirely sure of what I'm doing,” Matt said as Evan's hand encircled his wrist.

“We're doing okay, I think.”

They drank a pitcher of beer for old time's sake and ate their weight in wings. It didn't take as long as the old days—they both had somewhere they'd rather be.

Chapter Nineteen

"Evan Cerelli, good to meet you." The two people in Vic's semi-packed-up office rose to meet Evan as he stepped inside, the woman of the twosome clearly the senior person in charge as she spoke first. He could feel the eyes of the entire squad room watching the meeting through the half-glass wall; he could also feel his heart pulsing through his jacket.

"This is Aida Corzine and Richard Karz," Vic said, breaking the ice as best he could. He maneuvered between the pair and Evan.

Evan shook hands, then waited until the guests had taken their seats on the plaid sofa in the captain's office. He'd slept on that couch a few too many times. He'd sat there and wondered bleakly if his life and his career were over.

And now, the two people sitting on it wanted to make him an offer.

Vic sat in one of the visitors' chairs at his side.

"We've heard good things about you, Cerelli." Richard Karz had reportedly been a beat cop about a hundred and ten years ago, but no one had any real proof of that. He'd gone into politics and paperwork pretty soon after the academy. "Vic here hasn't stopped singing your praises."

Vic shrugged and snapped one of his suspenders. "Just because I haven't complained about him—doesn't mean I'm saying nice stuff all the time."

"I think that's exactly what it means." Aida had gone a more traditional route, if one could call being one of the first female Hispanic officers in the city's history traditional. She was looking at Evan like she could read his mind. He found it disconcerting, so he checked for lint on his pants to avoid her stare.

"Evan, I'm sure you have an inkling of what this is about," Vic said, taking the reins once again.

"I think so." Evan ventured a look at Aida and Richard, who were expectant and interested in the next part of the conversation. Clearly.

"With my retirement, everyone takes a step up. Spots open, things get shifted around…"

"He knows how it works," Richard smiled. "We're looking at you, Evan. May I call you Evan? We'd like you to take the captain's exam."

The gossip mills had been working overtime on this one for a while. To hear the actual words was a little overwhelming. A lot overwhelming. Moving from the practical hands-on to the political and managerial; it was something he had in mind over the years, he couldn't lie. It was good money, less danger.

That was a good combination.

It was also a huge commitment of his time.

"Thank you." Evan found his voice as quickly as he could, even as his thoughts tumbled and broke through his brain. "Thank you for considering me."

Aida looked at Richard, her perfect eyebrows meeting his in a raised pitch.

"Is that a yes?"

"I'd like to consider it for at least a day, speak to my..." And then Evan was full-stop stumped. They had to know his wife was dead; they had to know most everything about him. Hell, he couldn't imagine they didn't know about Matt.

Richard saved him from having to come up with a word. His slightly smarmy smile confirmed that they did indeed know about Matt. "You should definitely take some time to speak to your...family...about this. It's a big decision, of course. We wouldn't want you to make it lightly."

Evan cast a sidelong glance toward Vic.

"Can I ask a question?" He directed it back to the pair on the couch.

"Of course." That was Aida.

"Why me?"

There was the briefest of pauses that spoke volumes to Evan. Vic looked at his desk, coughed into his hand.

"You have an exemplary record, Detective. Commendations, letters of merit. High arrest rate."

"No different than my partner or half the detectives I know," Evan said, a calm coming over him.

"True. But it takes more than a record to make a good captain." Richard leaned forward, elbows on his knees.

"Very true. It takes a certain accumen of political savvy which I don't have." Evan matched Richard's position. "I've never expressed interest in going higher on the food chain here. I'm happy where I am."

"Is that a no?" Aida moved to the edge of the couch.

"No, it's not. I just want a straight answer."

Aida and Richard shared a sidelong glance, and Aida nodded slightly.

"You're a prime candidate because of your record and your…personal situation. We don't have enough diversity high up in the rankings, Evan. And you are perfect for what we're looking for." Aida smiled. "That's the truth."

"Not enough white guys in charge," Evan quipped, even as his palms began to sweat.

"Not enough gay men in charge." Richard threw the gauntlet down.

"I'm not…"

Aida waved her hand. "Bisexual, whatever the terminology you use. You live openly with another man, a former police officer. You're accepted by your fellow officers. It's the perfect situation."

Silence swelled in the office.

Vic coughed again, shifted in his seat.

"So what puts me over the edge in terms of the competition is that I live with another man?" The entire meeting was surreal, ironic. All that time he worried what being with Matt would do to his career, and now it was directing him to a promotion.

The singled-out part bothered him. A lot. He knew there was nothing at all wrong with his record or his ability. He knew he could become a good captain.

He didn't want to be known as the "gay" captain because someone needed a political quota.

"It's certainly a plus. We wouldn't be talking to you if the rest of your record wasn't exemplary." As he sat back, Richard gave him an appraising look. "You know you can do this. You know it would be good for people. Reverse stereotypes."

Evan opened his mouth to snap something, but he reined it in. Because he had as many stereotypes as the people Richard was talking about.

He had his own preconceived notions that he had fought against.

The reality of the situation was—he lived with a man. He was in love with a man, someone he trusted with the raising of his children. Gay, bisexual, formerly straight; words that didn't entirely encompass the situation.

"I'm not interested in being a symbol," Evan said finally. "If you'd like to evaluate me on the basis of my record, then please do. If the only winning point is me being bisexual, then I'd rather not have the job."

He gave Vic a nod, stood up and extended his hand to Aida and Richard. "Thank you. And good luck in finding your next captain."

Evan got collared by Helena as he walked out of Vic's office and all but thrown into an empty interrogation room.

"What the hell was that?" she said, the second after the door snicked closed.

"They're trying to fill a quota." Evan half laughed, half sighed as he threw himself into a chair. "They want a gay captain."

"And they picked you?" Helena grabbed a chair across from him, her jaw literally dropping.

"Is that surprising for some reason?"

"You're not exactly very out and…ohhhhhh." She nodded knowingly. "Gay but straight. They must've found out about you and started drooling."

"I'm not sure which part to be more horrified by, to be quite honest."

She gave him a semidisappointed look. "I know how much you hate being labeled…"

"I do, because you know—it shouldn't matter. But then it does, right? It matters to me." Evan wiped his forehead with the palm of his hand. "I get all indignant about being called gay, like it's wrong or hurtful or an insult. Meanwhile…" Evan sighed, thinking about all the fights he and Matt had been having lately. "Meanwhile, I go home every night to Matt."

"It bothers you that people know that."

Evan resisted the urge to bang his forehead against the table. "It shouldn't."

"It's scary, waiting for people to judge you."

"What if I'm judging myself? I fell in love. That's the bottom line. I wasn't looking, I wasn't exploring. I wasn't making a statement. I was drowning and I fell in love. Everything else is other people's shit."

"You're a lucky man. Lightning doesn't usually strike twice. Some of us are still waiting to get hit." Helena reached across the table to grab his hand. "I know things haven't been easy for you lately."

"I think I've been kind of a homophobe." Evan sighed.

"A bisexual homophobe. You just don't do anything easy, do you?"

"I also think I'm kind of a jerk sometimes."

"Can I plead the Fifth?"

"You know, as my best friend and partner, feel free to start defending my honor at any time."

"You say something I don't agree with, and I'll jump right in."

"Ooooo, burn."

"Jerk." Helena shook her head. "It's not like the world and society and people make it easy, Evan. To be gay or bi or single or whatever it is that isn't previously approved as the status quo. You're just a normal person—I hate to break this to you."

Evan smiled as he squeezed her fingers between his. "This shouldn't be the norm. My kids deserve better, Matt deserves better. Hell—so do I."

"You going to pursue the captain thing?"

"I told them to feel free to consider me for the job but I didn't want to be their token gay captain."

"Bisexual captain."

"Whatever. My love life shouldn't have any bearing on my job, unless I'm dating a pony."

"Um…ew."

"This is what I'm saying." Evan checked his watch. "We have to get back to work."

"When you're the boss, I want longer breaks."

His brain ticked and churned and returned to the conversation in Vic's office. He'd managed a few moments alone with his captain before he left, and Vic was apologetic for everything, but Evan thanked him. Sometimes he needed a kick in the ass.

Or ten.

Evan took the long way home; he didn't want to walk through the door and let his mouth convey something to Matt he didn't mean to.

Like he was ashamed of them. Like he didn't truly value their relationship.

Like somehow there was regret that they fell in love.

What had Helena said? Lightning didn't strike twice very often? He and Sherri, he and Matt. There were differences, of course, but in both relationships, Evan felt like the same person. The same worries, the same joys. Day to day changed, but God, day to day changed when he and Sherri were together. Teenagers in love don't compare to twins crying for bottles at three a.m.

Sherri didn't exactly compare to Matt, but Evan—Evan was the constant. And Evan was the only one who could make the necessary adjustments.

By the time he pulled up to the house, Evan felt the knot in his chest unraveling. His brain simmered down enough to pull into the garage without hitting the cans, and he sat for another second, two dueling thoughts in his head.

What was he going to say to Richard and Aida next time they asked about the captain track? And how was he going to go forward with Matt?

Step one was apparently getting out of the car.

The lights were on, the faint sound of the television filtering through to his ears as he walked up the front steps. For a moment he paused to look through the picture window and caught a glimpse of the kids sprawled around the living room. Katie was on the phone. The twins were watching television, each staking out one of the sofas as their own. Every light in the house seemed to be on, meaning Matt was attempting to cook dinner. Everything about the scene was inviting and comforting and home; for a second Evan worried he would have to take another lap around the neighborhood to keep the tears out of his eyes.

But Evan caught hold of his emotions and opened the door, stepping into the bright lights, volume on high version of the muted scene through window. It overwhelmed for a moment, then Evan smiled.

"Hey, Daddy," Elizabeth called from the sofa, curled in a sleepy ball as she gave him a wave.

He got a nod from Danny and one from Katie who continued her "Uh-huh, uh-huh, *oh my God*" litany into the cell.

Just a normal evening in the Cerelli/Haight household.

"I'm sorry, do I know you?" Matt called from the kitchen, using three kitchen towels to move a clearly steaming dish from the oven to the counter.

"I'm sorry, are you cooking?" Evan approached the kitchen warily.

"It might be a casserole."

"Might?"

Matt waved the steam away from the bubbling top. "There was a recipe on the back of the macaroni box."

Evan saw the table set for more than their usual number and started to worry he forgot something.

"Company?"

"Sorta." Matt leaned against the counter and gave Evan one of those patented wicked smiles of his. "We're hosting an impromptu prewedding bash."

"Bash?"

"Okay, casserole for you and me and the kids and Vic and Serena and Helena."

"Helena didn't mention…"

"Helena probably didn't know until her mother called her."

"Oh she'll be in a fun mood tonight."

Matt gave him a skewed look as he if were detecting an off odor. "What's up?"

"Weird day. I'll tell you later." He noticed then the huge arrangement of fruit and flowers on the counter. "What the heck is that?"

"Bennet and Daisy sent us a token of their appreciation or something like that. Look at the size of those apples. The size of a freaking cat."

"Why are they appreciative of us?"

"I have no idea. I was hoping you could explain manners in high society to me, because last I checked, I'm consulting and getting paid shitloads of money. Now I have giant fruit."

"I guess they're just being nice." Evan undid his tie. "I'm taking a shower before everyone gets here."

"Too late, headlights in the driveway. You smell fine."

"So, sorry about that earlier today," Vic said as Evan took his coat.

"Don't worry about it."

"I had plans tonight," Helena groused under her breath. "Did you talk to Matt about the job?"

"No, so be quiet," Evan said even as Vic's voice boomed from the kitchen.

"Captain?" he heard Matt say, and he sighed.

"Yeah, well, cat's out of the bag." Evan walked into the kitchen where Vic, Matt, and Serena stood. "It was just an inquiry to see if I was interested."

"Well shit," Matt said, his eyes wide. "That's amazing—congratulations."

"I take full credit," Vic smiled, clapping Evan on the shoulder.

"This is very exciting." Serena gave him a hug. "I feel like a torch is being passed."

Matt stared at Evan still, and Evan shrugged, smiled. "I have a long road to go, and it might not even happen."

"Think positively," Helena said, stealing bread off the table. "Someday soon you'll be hip deep in paperwork, having to go to meetings and conferences and eat bad chicken while you listen to budget recommendations." She smiled sweetly. "Try not to miss us little peons."

* * *

That night, Evan and Matt lay entwined in bed, sweaty and tired. They were getting better at the quiet, mind-blowing sex, thanks to a tireless attention to practice.

"Captain Cerelli, hmmm. You gonna get new dress blues?" Matt's voice was low, dirty.

Evan smirked. "Yeah."

"Looking forward to that."

"You can make anything perverted, can't you?"

"I try."

They were quiet for a few minutes, but Evan could feel the tension in Matt's body.

"What?"

Matt sighed. "I know you've thought about this, but if you do become captain, it's going to be tough to keep us a secret," he began.

Evan held up his hand.

"They know. It seems like it was a factor in them approaching me."

Matt whistled.

"And you're okay with that?"

"Define okay?"

"You're going along with it."

"I think I could be a decent captain." Evan shrugged. "I think I deserve to be considered."

"I'm beginning to think you got body snatched."

Evan sat up, looking down at Matt, his face serious.

"I'm just trying a lot harder than I was before. I don't want to waste my time anymore, Matt—I don't want to waste our time."

"Okay." Matt reached up and mock clocked him in the chin. "I believe you're really Evan Cerelli, and this is all really fucking amazing."

Chapter Twenty

A few weeks later

"Are you sure you have everything?" Matt intoned, his voice solemn and serious as he stood beside Evan in the foyer of the restaurant. "The ring, your prepared toast?"

Evan rolled his eyes. "Shut up and stop trying to make me nervous."

"I'm making you nervous?" Matt sounded delighted. Evan forgave him his glee only because he looked obscenely good in his dark blue suit and polka-dotted tie.

"You have a job to do too, you know…" Evan surreptitiously felt around in his own navy suit pocket for the ring box and index card of notes.

"I'm pretty sure I can handle being charming and telling fifty people where to sit," he said. A nearby antique mirror drew him over for another quick hair and tie check. "Forgot my riot gear, though."

"Just do me a favor and make sure the kids don't run amuck."

"The kids not running amuck is my full-time job, soon-to-be Lieutenant Cerelli. And I'm fairly brilliant at it."

Evan smiled; he slipped his hand into Matt's and didn't even check over his shoulder to see who might be watching. "Yes. Yes, you are."

"Plus I gave them each twenty bucks to behave."

Evan sighed. "Twenty?"

"Katie negotiated." Matt shrugged. "We probably need to start saving for law school with that one."

It was such an uncomplicated, natural domestic moment that Evan squeezed Matt's hand in lieu of words. Matt smiled back, not quite understanding judging by the look in his eyes.

"Good thing you got that glamorous security job."

"Consulting must be Latin for shitload of money, not a lot of work." Matt grinned. He gestured toward the closed front doors of the restaurant with his shoulder. "Should I go out and start directing people inside?"

Evan checked his watch. "Might as well. I have to go find Vic and make sure he's ready."

"Don't offer to help him climb out a window or anything. If he says yes, Helena is going to wring your neck." Matt laughed at his own joke, bussing a kiss on Evan's check before disengaging their hands and heading for the heavy double doors.

"I wouldn't do that," Evan said; he knew Matt was teasing, but still… "And he wouldn't say yes."

Matt looked toward the ceiling in exasperation. "Kidding. Really. Even a bachelor like me knows true love when he sees it." He fluttered his eyelashes, teasing, but Evan shook his head.

“You're not a bachelor anymore,” he said simply. Matt stopped in between the doorway, the sun shining brightly behind him.

“Oh,” Matt said lightly. “That's a good point.”

They shared a look, long and meaningful, and Evan sincerely wished the wedding was over and the reception was finished and they were back in that nice hotel room Vic had graciously gifted them with this weekend.

“I'm gonna go…you know, fulfill my duties as an usher.” Matt smiled. He half waved, then disappeared into the light, the door snicking closed behind him.

Evan rocked back on his heels, his hands dug deep in his pockets.

He was a married man again, for all intents and purposes. The slim gold band that represented his marriage to Sherri sat on his dresser; he didn't think he and Matt were the “commitment ceremony” type, but Evan felt very secure in the fact that Matt wasn't going anywhere and neither was he.

He doubted the kids would stand for it. He doubted if either he or Matt could conceive of it.

And now he had traditional-type marriage things to do—like give Vic a pep talk about how the second time around could mean just as much as the first.

Vic, as it turned out, wasn't very nervous. Neither was Serena. They stood in front of the floor-to-ceiling windows, with the bright sunlight surrounding them, staring into each other's eyes as the judge made everything legal. There was a general sniffling from the gathered guests. Evan kept dry-eyed but there was a moment during the "I do's" when he peeked over at Matt—sitting with the kids in the front row—and smiled, feeling sentimental.

Miranda caught the look and made a gagging gesture.

Then she and Matt traded elbows to the ribs, as sure a gesture as a hug when it came to those two.

Evan was touched. The judge pronounced Serena and Vic husband and wife, and the hired violinist hit her perfect cue as the applause broke out.

Helena clutched his arm tightly as they walked down to the back of the makeshift aisle. She sniffled against his shoulder as he patted her hand.

"Okay?" he asked quietly.

"Yes. Just officially melancholy." Helena wiped a few stray tears away with her wrist, hiding the motion behind her bouquet of tightly wrapped lavender roses. "Mom and Vic look so happy."

Evan watched the newlyweds stopping at every row to collect hugs and congratulations. They both glowed, and even as they turned apart to accept good wishes, their hands were tightly clenched.

"They do. And you look great in violet. Like a young Liz Taylor," he teased.

Helena gave him a light punch in the arm. "Shut up." She looked over the crowd—now moving toward the adjoining room for cocktails—and saw Matt herding the kids together. "Matt's coming over here. Everything okay with you guys?"

Evan smiled in the direction of his approaching family. "Things are good actually."

"You decided about becoming my boss?"

"I could say something about always being the boss of you, but I value my life."

"Good man."

"But actually—yes. I'm going to say yes."

"Even if they want to make you their manly gay poster boy for captains?"

Evan shrugged. "I accept that I'm going to have to deal with the political shit. But I think I can be a good captain and…" He paused, catching Matt's eye as he reached them. "I think I can be a good role model."

"Are we discussing your dapper usage of pocket hankies? Because really man, good stuff," Matt said, moving past Evan to give Helena a kiss on the cheek.

"No, we're discussing how your boyfriend is going to be my boss, and I expect serious favoritism." Helena smiled, wrapping her arm around Matt's waist.

Evan clucked his tongue disapprovingly.

Miranda and Katie, having said some brief hellos to his partner, had already pulled out their cell phones, and the twins wandered over toward the incredible pull of fancy party food and fruity drinks.

"Can you girls take Elizabeth and Danny in to get something to eat?" Evan asked.

"I have to make a phone call," Miranda started, lifting her eyes from the miniscreen briefly to catch her father's glare. “Which I will make after I see that the precious tweens get their share of the stuffed mushrooms.”

“Good call.”

“She's going to ask you for money when you drop her off later,” Katie interjected, artfully dodging her older sister's scowl and swipe.

“I have no doubt,” Evan said. “Although I already know she got money from Matt.”

“We did too!” Elizabeth said happily, patting the pocket of her shiny satin skirt. Danny nodded; he was too busy taking off his tie and stuffing it in his back pocket to contribute much more.

“We need to have a family conference about you paying them off,” Evan said to Matt.

“I have expenses.” Miranda put her cell back into her purse and gestured the twins toward the other room. “Come on. Let's go before all the good stuff is gone.”

“You're underage, no drinking,” Matt called helpfully.

“I'll make sure she doesn't.” Sweet Katie, always so helpful. Always so evil.

Miranda made a sound of frustration and herded the twins through the waiters folding up the chairs. Katie trailed after, a look of delight written on her face.

“Sweet kids,” Helena said drily.

“If anyone deserves extreme favoritism from your partner, it's me. I turned down a glamorous bodyguard job for all this.”

“You get sex, and I get him at his grumpiest. How is that fair?”

Matt shook his head. "It sounds cheap when you put it that way."

"Standing right here." Evan sighed. Maybe he needed to check out the stuffed mushroom situation on his own and get away from the teasing.

"I need a drink," Helena announced, apropos of nothing. "Maybe two. My mother got married before I did!"

"You know, it generally happens that way, Helena." Evan took her other arm, taking a swat in the face with her bouquet as she gestured wildly.

"I know but in *my* case—which we're actually talking about here—she got married *first* for the *first* time." Helena shook her head. "I'm a spinster!"

"Oh God, how drunk are you going to get?" Matt asked.

"Listen, I was thinking. If I'm not married by forty, I'm going to need sperm from one of you…"

Evan managed to get Helena a drink and set her up to dance with one of Vic's nephews—who was twenty-something, single, and clearly eager to dance with his gorgeous partner. He made her swear not to mention spinsterhood or donating sperm as the young man led her away.

She swore.

He checked on the kids—more teens on cell phones, more tweens eating their weight in shrimp—then grabbed a bottled beer from the bartender. By the time Evan found Matt shooting the shit in the corner with Lenny, he was working a full-on sweat.

"Do I have to keep the jacket on for the toast?" he asked, collapsing into a chair near where the men were sitting.

Lenny snickered. "Yeah, sorry, man. Jacket, tie, slightly crushed rose…"

Evan looked down his boutonniere which seemed as worse for the wear as he felt.

"Crap. I'm glad we took the pictures before." He opened his beer and took a long sip, stretching his legs out. "This best man thing is hard work."

"Wait till you're father of the bride," Matt quipped.

"At least I'll have help with that," Evan answered, giving him a pointed look.

Lenny laughed out loud. "Matty'll probably buy 'em a ladder and give 'em enough for airfare to Vegas."

"Shhhhh." Matt elbowed him.

"No," Evan said slyly. "He's a closet romantic."

"Shhhhh," Matt said again, glancing into his empty glass. "Don't ruin my rep, guys, please." He gestured with the glass and headed for the bar.

"He looks good," Lenny said, as Matt wove his way through the dancing crowd. "Happy."

Evan felt like blushing, but he nodded at his boyfriend's old partner. "Yeah."

Lenny sipped his club soda as he looked through the crowd. "Never saw him like that before."

"Well." Evan coughed. He fussed with his jacket. "We're, uh—things are going well for us. It wasn't, uh—expected. But it's worked out."

"Hmm," Lenny responded, still looking thoughtfully toward the bar where Matt was becoming fast friends with the bartender.

Evan wanted to leave it alone, but the hmm was too cryptic not to respond to. "Hmmm?"

Lenny chuckled. "Are you gonna interrogate me now?"

"Maybe." Evan leaned back in the chair and gave the retired detective his best level stare. "I'm curious about your take on all this. You were probably closest to Matt over pretty much anyone else."

"Before you."

"Before me."

"Well…" Lenny munched on a sliver of ice from his nearly empty glass. "Matt was all about the job. It was his wife, his mistress—no one else got much of his time, you know."

"So—basically your average cop."

Lenny chuckled. "Right. But without an outlet. Hell, not even a wife or an addiction to give him a break." The words were lighthearted, but Evan got the underlying message.

"He was a little lost when we met." Evan dropped his voice slightly, as the music and festivities swelled up around them. "So was I, for that matter."

"He needed something to focus on, something healthier than being a cop." Lenny shifted in his seat. He glanced over his shoulder—as did Evan—to make sure no one was close enough to be eavesdropping. There were plenty of cops on the guest list and most of them knew Matt and Evan both.

"This is almost a Hallmark moment." Evan admired the shine on his shoes, then looked up to see the kind expression on Lenny's face.

"Eh, I'll deny every word of it."

"This never even happened."

Evan looked to the dance floor to spot Matt dancing a mock tango with the jubilant bride. He wasn't the least bit surprised.

"I should feel guilty for being so fortunate," Evan said quietly. He knew Lenny was watching Matt same as he was. "I honestly don't know how I would have made it without him."

"I think he likes that."

Evan smiled. "Yeah, I think so. He loves being the glue. It's a crazy job to volunteer for."

"I think it's the best job for him." Lenny shrugged, as if it were the most obvious thing in the world. "Plus, not sure if you picked up on this, but Matty doesn't do anything half-way. It's one percent or a thousand percent."

"Yeah," Evan drawled thoughtfully. "Yeah, I noticed that. What's the nice way you put it? He's, uh—focused."

Lenny snickered. "You just give him the assignment, tell him he's good at it, and you'll get the best of Matt Haight, and that's—that's pretty damn good."

Evan smiled. He knew Lenny was right, and it felt nice to have his validation. Matt had no real family beyond the guys on the force who stayed loyal, like Lenny and Vic, or Liz, another friend from his cop days. Sometimes he forgot that when it came down to it, their little family (kids and friends) were all either of them had.

"Thanks, Lenny."

"No problem, kid."

Evan laughed at the "kid" moniker. "You should come over for dinner some time. Matt would love it."

"You just tell me, then. Old retired guys like me can't turn down a home-cooked meal."

"Matt's been experimenting lately," Evan looked dubious.

"I'll settle for home ordered."

"Done." They shook hands, and Evan got up to join the rest of the party.

The clinking of spoons against glasses signaled another round of kisses; Vic and Serena puckered up and smooched as applause rocked the restaurant. Evan watched from the back of the room, sipping a bit of champagne and girding his nerves before entering the spotlight. He had a speech to deliver.

A whistling Matt swayed up to him, a tiny sheen on his face the only real clue he'd been dancing for hours now.

"I had no idea you were secretly Fred Astaire."

"Me neither! It started with Serena and then bam—I think I've danced with every female here. Except Miranda." He made an amused face, settling next to Evan against the wall. "I'm going to keep asking her, though."

"Because it annoys her."

"Of course! Why else would I do it?"

Evan looked to the corner where his children were sitting with some of Vic's nieces and nephews. Sometimes he had to blink when he saw them in moments like this, to erase the image of helpless babies and reckless toddlers and focus on the young women (and man) they were becoming.

Daunting.

"Thank God I have you here to help me with them," Evan murmured, thinking about his conversation with Lenny earlier.

"Uh—okay. You're welcome." Matt flushed beside him, hands digging deep into his suit pockets. "You know I love it, right?"

"Of course."

"And I'm gonna keep doing it."

"What happens when Elizabeth and Danny go off to college?"

Matt looked slightly horrified. "That's like—nine years away! Stop rushing it."

Evan smothered a laugh at the panicked expression on Matt's face. "Sorry. You're right. Eons away."

"Eons. Jeez. They can barely function without me," Matt huffed.

Evan humored him as he pulled the index cards from his pocket. "You turned down a lot of money, though."

"I have my pension. It's not like we're hurting." Matt crossed his arms over his chest. "Plus you're getting a big fat raise real soon, Captain Cerelli."

"Jumping the gun there."

"It'll happen."

"We'll see."

"It will."

"Okay, then."

They stood shoulder to shoulder for a few moments; then Evan surprised them both by leaning over and stealing a kiss.

"I'll be right back," he said smoothly, fighting a tiny blip of nerves at being affectionate in public.

Nothing terrible happened as he strode up the microphone, and the music simmered down to a quiet bit of background.

"Hi everyone, my name is Evan Cerelli." He cleared his throat gently. "I'm the best man as you might have already surmised, and I—Well, I'd like to thank you all on behalf of Serena and Vic and their families for being here today." A smattering of applause gave him a second of pause. His eyes sought Matt out, still resting against the back wall of the room.

He left the cards in his pocket.

"I feel today we've witnessed something—hopeful, optimistic. Maybe even more so than the usual wedding. We're young, we're just starting out, we have so many hopes and dreams. And then—well, life happens. Sometimes we find ourselves down a road we didn't imagine. Maybe even alone." Evan took a deep breath, smiling over at Vic and Serena. "Maybe we've given up on being so optimistic and hopeful until one day, a person comes into your life who breathes an energy back into it. Who gives you a whole new way to look at a life you were certain held no more surprises."

Evan raised his glass to the happy couple. "Vic and Serena, everyone here is blessed to know you, separately and together. We're all fortunate to witness this new part of your lives, to share in your happiness and your enthusiasm and your love. And this continuation of happily ever after. Thank you."

Raised glasses and murmurs of agreement filled the room; Vic and Serena raised their glasses first to Evan, then the room.

"Thank you," Serena said.

Everyone toasted the bride and groom, sealing the ritual with a sip of sparkling champagne.

Evan ducked out of the spotlight as the music kicked up a bit louder, escaping to where he'd left Matt.

"You're a sap," his boyfriend said, smiling and maybe just a bit more bright-eyed than when Evan left.

"Yeah." Evan closed the space between them and leaned in again—less surprising and more necessary than the time before. "Yeah, I am."

Their lips touched, and Evan felt his heart swell with the reality of his words, in his own life.

THE END

Tere Michaels

Tere Michaels began her writing career at the age of four when her mother explained that people made their living by making up stories—*and* they got paid. She got out her crayons and paper and never looked back. Many pages and crayons later—she eventually graduated to typewriters and then computers—Tere has article clips from major magazines, a thousand ideas still left to write and a family in the suburbs. She's exceedingly pleased every time someone reads her stories and cries, laughs or just feels happy.

Keep up with Tere at http://www.teremichaels.com.